"I wasn't the one wanted to be a preacher."

Don't get me wrong—most days I really like my pa. I wouldn't trade him for anyone else's, even the Westons', who owns half of Leonardstown and has bought them both brand-new bicycles. But land o' Goshen, why did I have to be a preacher's boy?

It isn't just Pa. The whole town thinks they got a right to tell me how to behave. People just have unrealistic expectations if your pa happens to be a preacher. One: You are supposed to be clean—all the time, not just on Sundays. And Two: You are supposed to be good. I don't have a talent for either—nor wish to.

ALSO BY KATHERINE PATERSON

Preacher's Boy

Katherine Paterson

HarperTrophy®
An Imprint of HarperCollinsPublishers

For
Carter Lord Paterson
and
Griffin Loomis Paterson,
who are not preacher's boys,
and
for their fathers, who were

Harper Trophy® is a registered trademark of
HarperCollins Publishers Inc.

Preacher's Boy
Copyright © 1999 by Minna Murra, Inc.
Printed in the United States of America.
For information address HarperCollins Children's Books,
a division of HarperCollins Publishers, 1350 Avenue of the Americas,
New York, NY 10019.

Library of Congress Cataloging-in-Publication Data
Paterson, Katherine.
  Preacher's boy / Katherine Paterson.
    p. cm.
  Summary: In 1899, ten-year-old Robbie, son of a preacher in a small Vermont town, gets
himself into all kinds of trouble when he decides to give up being Christian in order to
make the most of his life before the end of the world.
  ISBN 0-06-447233-7
  [1. Family life—Vermont—Fiction. 2. Fathers and sons—Fiction. 3. Christian life—
Fiction. 4. Vermont—Fiction.] I. Title.
PZ7.P273Pr 2001   00-031964
[Fic]—dc21

Typography by Henrietta Stern
❖
First Harper Trophy edition, 2001
Visit us on the World Wide Web!
www.harperchildrens.com

Preacher's Boy

How the Trouble Began

On Decoration Day, while everyone else in town was at the cemetery decorating the graves of our Glorious War Dead, Willie Beaner and me, Robert Burns Hewitt, took Mabel Cramm's bloomers and run them up the flagpole in front of the town hall. That was the beginning of all my troubles.

It wasn't that we got caught. In fact, I've often thought since *that* would have been the best thing in the world. If we'd been caught, Pa, who is a preacher and therefore has to be in favor of repentance, would have made us both apologize to Mabel, brought me home, and given me a good hiding—or as good a hiding as Pa can manage. He never can put his heart into corporal punishment—a weakness often lamented by Deacon Slaughter. In the rest of the town there would have been a few days' worth of people cutting their eyes sidewise at us, but in a couple of weeks—say, by the middle of June—the whole affair would've been forgotten.

As it was, by the middle of June the boys—well, they

act like boys even if they are the size of men—the boys that hang around the livery stable were still speculating as to who had had the nerve to do it "in broad daylight, mind you!" and then slapping their knees and snorting like horses.

I still think Mabel herself is due part of the blame. Everyone returned from the cemetery that morning to discover a foreign object streaming just below Old Glory. It was quickly evident that the object fluttering in the spring breeze was a pair of female unmentionables, so Deacon Slaughter and Mr. Weston (being the leading citizens) conferred and decided the said unmentionables should be lowered and handed over to the sheriff for decent disposal. But when those bloomers got to eye level, Mabel Cramm had no more sense than to shriek out like a banshee, "They're mine!" Whereupon she fainted dead away. From that moment, Chaos took charge and Rumor reigned.

And it wasn't just those loafers at the stable; the whole goldurn town was aflutter. Mothers were keeping their daughters indoors, except for Mabel's mother, who had bundled her off on the afternoon train that very day to visit her grandmother in Waterbury until she recovered her equilibrium or the culprit was found and punished, whichever came first.

With all the fuss, there was no way Willie and me could confess. If we'd been caught, which by all rights we should have been, we'd've been tanned and sent to bed without our supper, and the whole thing dismissed as a schoolboy prank. Which it was. I swear. We were just trying to keep up with Tom and Ned Weston.

Two weeks before, the Weston boys had put a green snake into Teacher's lunch pail. It made a lovely to-do. All those girls screaming and putting their hands over their eyes and jumping up on their desks. Miss Bigelow didn't scream, but you could tell she wanted to and was barely keeping herself in line. You could see in her eyes the war between screaming and staying calm so she could quiet those hysterical girls.

Funny thing about that. It was only the older town girls. The farm girls and the little girls didn't scream at all. To tell the truth, they were just as interested in studying the varmint as the boys. It was only the girls practicing to be young ladies who went berserk and threatened to expire. I'll never understand women. No, it's not the whole kit 'n' kaboodle of the ladylike female race. Nobody beats my ma in the ladylike department, and she never once in my lifetime went silly over a snake or a mouse either. We have plenty of mice running through that rattletrap manse where we live. Ma just gets a broom and chases them back to their holes.

But I'm getting off the subject. Tom and Ned never got caught. Only Willie and me saw the whole thing, and we aren't squealers. Tom and Ned were well aware of this. It made them act even more superior to us than usual, which me and Willie could not tolerate. So we figured that the only thing we could do is think up something even more outrageous and get away with it. Only we'd be smarter than them. We'd not even let Tom and Ned see us. Then they wouldn't know for *sure* we'd done it. They'd just go crazy wondering over it.

See, if they knew for sure, then they'd have to think up something even worse and not let anybody but us know. And then Willie and me would be obliged to think up something still worse, and so on and so on until we were all four dead or too old to care, one or the other.

"Now, the hardest part," I explained to Willie, "is that we can't brag. Not by the flicker of the eyebrow, you understand?"

"No," he said. "How do you flicker an eyebrow?"

"It's a manner of speaking," I said, prim as a school-marm.

"Wal, why would I want to brag anyway?"

"You wouldn't, normally. But the thing is—human nature being what it is—we're going to be fair busting with the desire to hint to the Weston boys that we were the ones who pulled this off."

The actual crime was easy to commit. On Monday, the twenty-ninth of May, which was the day before Decoration Day, we watched, hidden in the tall grass, while the Cramms' hired girl hung out the wash behind their house. She was careful, as all women are, to hang the bloomers and other unmentionables in between the other things, but we were watching sharp, and when we saw the

4

Mabel-sized pink bloomers pegged to the line, we took note.

"Write it down, Private Beaner," I said. "Right between the brown skirt and the pink shirtwaist."

"Private? Who's private?"

"Ah, Willie, somebody's got to be private or it ain't a scouting mission."

"Then what are you, Robbie?"

I rather fancied cap'n or major, but I could tell from the look on Willie's face that neither of those was likely to go down too well. "Sergeant," I said. "The sergeant has the private write stuff down."

"I ain't got nothing to write with," he said grumpily.

"*Pretend,* Willie. Write it down in your head."

He gave me that kind of patient look he gives when I want to pretend we're fighting in a war. Well, can you blame me? I wasn't born when they fought the Great War to End the Oppression of Slavery, and when they were sending troops to avenge the *Maine* and free the Cubans from Spanish tyranny, I was only nine years old. I don't think there's ever going to be a war I can really fight in.

"I can't write nothing down in my head. My whole forehead's turned to granite trying to keep my blamed eyebrows from flickering."

I gave up. We waited without whispering until we saw the hired girl go out the door with her basket, headed for the meat market and the general store. We'd already made sure the family had gone off somewhere. That's why we picked Cramms'. We didn't have any grudge against Mabel—no more grudge, that is, than we have against most girls. We crept down the hill, pinched just the one pair of bloomers, and tidied the line to cover the spot. The bloomers were still damp, but I carried them in my hand all the way up the hill to our secret place deep in the woods—an act which I considered fairly brave, but which Willie gave me no credit for at all.

Willie's and my place used to be someone's cabin, but the last owner left fifty or more years ago, probably headed west. In those days lots of people left Vermont, just up and deserted their hill farms, looking for an easier life on the plains. Woods have grown up now where pasture and fields had once been. It's a bit spooky, that tumbledown cabin. But once Willie and me stumbled on it, we knew it was the perfect place for us. We can hide away there from the Weston boys and anyone else that aggravates us. Sometimes we read dime novels there that Ma never wants to see the likes of around the manse. Sometimes we talk. Sometimes we just go there to do nothing but get away from stuff at home.

We have a lot to get away from, Willie and me. Willie's folks died when he was a baby, so he lives with his aunt Millie. She isn't really mean, and she's too arthritic to chase him up a mountain, but she does like to make the boy work around the house and garden. Willie even washes dishes. She gets cranky as an old hen when she thinks he's slacking off.

I don't have to do women's work. I have Ma and Beth, who's fifteen and practicing hard at being grown up. Then there's Letty, who's only five but who always loves to think she's helping. And . . . Elliot. It's hard to tell you about Elliot. If you could see him . . . But you can't. He's almost two years older than me and about a foot taller, but, well, Elliot's simple in the head. That's the best I can explain it.

One of the worst fights I ever had with the Weston boys was because they were picking on Elliot. It was right after church one Sunday. The grownups were hanging around chatting like usual. A bunch of us boys had gone over to the horse sheds to see the horses. The farmers' horses are pretty much old friends, since we see them Sunday after Sunday in the sheds, where they are waiting patiently for their owners to get out of church and get them home for dinner.

Willie and me were doing acrobatics on a shed door when over from the churchyard we heard Ned Weston say, "Hello, there, Elliot. How's tricks?" We knew he meant nothing but trouble, but Elliot loves everyone. He didn't know he was being picked on.

"Sing us a song, Elliot," says Tom.

"Yeah, big fellow," Ned chimes in. "Sing us a song!"

Me and Willie slid off the shed door and went to see what was happening. If your pa's the preacher, you know a lot of hymns, even if you're slow. Elliot started singing his favorite—"What a Friend We Have in Jesus"—only

Elliot slides his words, so it comes out something like "Wha a fen we ha in Sheeshush." Elliot was singing along happily, and the Westons joined in, both of them shuffling their feet and walking around with their right shoulders lower than their left and copying Elliot's way of making his words, so the next line comes out "Aw our shins and grease to bear." They were holding their stomachs to keep from laughing.

Elliot was smiling away. Other boys don't usually play with him, and here was Tom and Ned Weston, the sons of the richest man in town, heaping all this attention on him, smiling and singing his favorite song along with him.

I walked up and whacked Ned Weston in the face. "Hey, you!" he yelled. Then his big brother, Tom, jumped in. They were both on me, knocking me to the ground. Willie would have jumped in, too, but I called him off. It was my fight, not his. The Westons probably would have beat me senseless, two on one like that, but Elliot stopped singing and started yelling for Pa.

Pa came running off the church porch and saved my life. I was not grateful. It just made the Westons feel even more superior that I had to be saved by my "big old papa." Pa waded into the fracas and hoisted me up right off the ground by the back of my shirt. There I hung with my legs dangling in the air. I could see his eyes flashing, and I thought for a minute he was going to wallop me. Instead he lets me down gentle. "Oh, Robbie," he says, "when are you going to learn to settle things with your head instead of your fists?"

At that point I could see the Westons doubled over trying not to laugh out loud in front of the preacher. Pa couldn't have humiliated me more if he'd yanked down my britches and paddled my bare bottom right there in the churchyard. I couldn't understand why he didn't leave me alone to fight my own fights. A boy has got to learn to take up for himself in this world. I couldn't walk away from a fight. It would ruin my reputation.

Besides, a lot of my fights in those days were because of Elliot. You'd think Pa would admire the fact that I was willing to get my nose bloodied for Elliot's sake. But no, he thought I should let those ignorant Westons call me a yellow-livered coward and never raise a finger. All because I was born to be his son.

Pa hates any kind of fighting. It's because he can remember the Great War, though just barely. His father fought in it. They were living in Massachusetts then. Pa says what he remembers is how much grieving the womenfolk did, and how, when his pa came home, everyone was laughing and crying at the same time. He says he couldn't understand, being only four years old, why his mother should be laughing and crying and all because of some stranger. It didn't make sense to him.

Pa started talking about all the pain and sorrow that the Civil War caused when everyone was yelling and hollering that President McKinley should hurry up and send troops to get the goldurned Spanish out of Cuba; Pa didn't like it one little bit. In fact, he said in church one Sunday right in the sermon that war was Hell, and he thought it broke the heart of God to see His children killing and maiming each other.

Deacon Slaughter rose up from his pew kind of slow like and marched down the aisle and clean out the door. Willie, who is my spy in the world at large, says that Deacon Slaughter told Mr. Weston that the Reverend Hewitt needed to learn a bit more about Hell before he went to throwing the term around. For once in my life I was inclined to agree with Deacon Slaughter.

Don't get me wrong—most days I really like my pa. I wouldn't trade him for anyone else's, even the Westons', who owns half of Leonardstown and has bought them both brand-new bicycles. But land o' Goshen, why did I have to be a preacher's boy?

It isn't just Pa. The whole town thinks they got a right to tell me how to behave. People just have unrealistic expectations if your pa happens to be a preacher. One: You are supposed to be clean—all the time, not just on Sundays. And Two: You are supposed to be good. I don't have a talent for either—nor wish to.

I wasn't the one wanted to be a preacher. It was Pa, and he's clean and good enough for eight or ten people. They should be plenty satisfied with that and not go laying impossible demands on his offspring.

Of course, Beth is clean and good in the way girls her

age tend to be. Which makes her a pain in the neck to me and a joy and comfort to the rest of the world. No one's keeping score on Letty yet. She's still a baby to their way of thinking. Poor Elliot. I guess he's kind of in the baby category, too. So it is always and only me that gets the pursed lips and tut-tuts and "Robbie, you of all people! And your father a minister!"

All right, back to the problem of Mabel Cramm's bloomers. No one got caught. There was mighty speculation, as I think I've said, down at the livery stable. Neither Willie nor me was privy to those conversations, but I think I can assure you that our names never came up in that sniggering talk.

The ladies of Leonardstown were noisily appalled, and whatever their menfolk might have thought privately, there was a general agreement, at least among the members of our Congregational church, that it was yet another evidence of the creeping moral decay that was rotting America from the core like a worm in an apple. Previously, they had been able to look down their noses at the other forty-four states, but America's worm had invaded the Green Mountains of Vermont and crawled all the way into our beautiful little village.

In addition to the shocking affair of the flying bloomers, there was the rowdy crowd that hung around the livery stable. They weren't just talking horseflesh, that was plain. You don't do that much snorting and knee slapping discussing gait and coat and size of livery-stable mares and geldings.

And then there were the Italian stonecutters. Now, the Italians go to the Catholic church in Tyler if they go anywhere at all, and in my opinion that isn't any business of the old-time New England Protestant population. But while the pious folks were on the subject of wickedness, they started in on the Italian population as well. Those men were drinking something considerably harder than the local cider—and none of them even pretended it was for medicinal purposes. Everyone knew that certain of the Italian women brewed their own, so to speak. But in a state that enshrined prohibition as law, maybe it was high time the sheriff stopped looking the other way.

And getting closer to home, there was the current preacher at the Congregational church. Whether you were Methodist, Baptist, Unitarian, or nothing at all, you still looked to the tall white steeple on Main Street as a symbol of purity and piety come from Heaven straight down to earth. There was, it was noted, a certain lack of rigor in the current occupant. According to the going opinion, he was a good man, but he was far too easy on sin.

Then I had to go and make matters worse. I was sitting with Willie in the evening service. Ma knows it is a burden for me to have to go to church twice on Sundays, and Wednesday-night prayer meeting to boot, so sometimes she lets me sit with Willie, making me promise to behave. Willie's aunt's pew is right behind the Westons'.

I was behaving, just like I promised, but fate intervened.

The church was stuffy as a coffin. What was I doing in church on such a night? My mind drifted miles away. I was a sweating private on the lines waiting for Johnny Reb to show the whites of his eyes over the rise. The rise being Mrs. Weston's back, which is about as broad as East Hill. Boy, it was hot. I pulled out one of the pew fans from the rack in front of me and begun to flap a little breeze toward my sweaty face. That was when I saw it. Right in the middle of the sermon, there was a large black spider crawling up that generous expanse of brown silk, heading for Mrs. Weston's high-necked collar.

I punched Willie with the fan, and we both watched fascinated to see how far the spider would get before Mrs. Weston knew it was there and what would happen if and when it got to the top of her collar. Well, what happened was it crept right up that stiff collar, teetered, and was about to get its balance and ruin all our fun. So I leaned over as if in prayer, and, delicate as a Civil War surgeon removing a bullet, put the edge of the fan under the spider's four lower legs and tipped it right down the back of Mrs. Weston's dress.

At first, Mrs. Weston just twitched a bit, but before long she began wiggling like a caterpillar when you tickle it with a stick. And the way she wiggled and pawed, you had to figure that the creature had made its way around to the front and was exploring the territory on the other side of the world. I tried to control myself, but before I knew it, a livery-stable-sized snort just popped right out of my mouth. That got Willie going and only made matters worse.

Suddenly I realized that there was silence where there should have been preaching. I felt it before I looked up. There standing at my elbow in the aisle was the tall form of my father. He wasn't saying a word. He was just looking at me. Nobody ever sobered up as fast as I did that night. Pa never said a thing. He just marched back up the aisle, climbed the stairs to the platform, and took up preaching where he left off, leaving my face as red as the side of a new-painted barn. While every eye was on Pa, Mrs. Weston seized the opportunity to escape down the aisle and out the door.

It doesn't make much sense to me even now, but that night I raced home—the manse is just up the hill behind the church—ran up two flights of stairs to Elliot's and my bedroom, and climbed under the quilt. I guess I was hoping if Pa didn't see me right off, he'd forget the whole incident. It was Elliot, not Pa, who came looking for me.

"Oooo, Robbie, you in big trouble."

I stuck my head under the pillow. I was in no mood to deal with Elliot.

"You scare', Robbie?"

"No, I am not scare'."

"Den why you hidin'?"

I threw back the covers and jumped out of bed. "I'm not hiding, you dummy! Just go away and leave me alone, will you?" He stood there with his mouth open, looking more dumb than ever, which made me yell all the louder. "Get outta here," I said. "Take your stupid self out of my sight!"

"What is going on up here?" Pa was standing in the doorway. He's so tall, he has to stoop a little or bump his head on the doorjamb when he comes into our bedroom, which is under the eaves.

I shut up yelling pretty quick. He was staring at me something fierce, but I didn't want him to think I was as ashamed as I felt, so I made myself look him in the eyes.

He turned toward Elliot. "Elliot," he said quietly, "please go downstairs. I need to talk to Robbie a minute."

Elliot smiled his sweet silly smile. "'kay, Pa." Sometimes that smile could drive me near crazy.

Pa waited until Elliot had clumped down the stairs. "Well, Robbie," he said, "I don't know where to begin."

I just sniffed. I was still furious, though I couldn't have told you who I was mad at.

He waited a minute, but when he realized I wasn't going to say anything, he went on. "I'm less concerned about your behavior in church than I am about your behavior just now toward your brother."

I shrugged my shoulders. Nobody needed to tell me I shouldn't have yelled that way at Elliot. But I didn't want him saying so.

I guess he realized that it wasn't the time for a lecture on Elliot. "As for your behavior in church—"

"I don't know why I always got to go to church—"

"Because you're a member of this family."

"Nobody asked me about that."

"Oh, Robbie—" I could tell he wanted to say more, but he was too exasperated and hurt to keep at it. "When you're ready to talk in a sensible fashion, I'll be in my study."

I showed him. I never went downstairs until the next morning.

Preparing for the End of the Age

N one of the church people ever spoke of my behavior that night. They would see me coming and shake their heads, but they'd done that for years. It was Pa's reputation that got further damaged, not mine. A preacher who couldn't prevent his own son from disrupting divine services was lacking proper authority even in his own household, they said. They all felt it would have helped if Pa had had the moral fortitude to lay a rod across my rear once a day and twice on Saturdays.

But I wasn't the only problem, they said. The sermons themselves lacked passion. They asked each other when was the last time the word *Hell* had been thundered from the pulpit? Calling war "Hell" didn't seem to count. It occurred to them that they hadn't heard more than a thimbleful of fiery damnation since the Reverend J. K. Pelham left town twelve years previously to take a larger charge in western Connecticut. No wonder the town was about to disappear down the broad path of turpitude and outright wickedness. All that drinking and obscene thinking and flying you-know-whats from the town hall flagpole—no one was warning the citizenry about the wrath to come.

Folks began to wax near nostalgic about those good old days. Why, Reverend Pelham's sermons would make tears come to the ladies' eyes and the sweat break out on the foreheads of grown men. Oh, that those mighty days should return. So the deacons determined to write to Reverend Pelham and invite him home to Leonardstown to preach on what they were calling "Revival Sunday." They figured a good dose of the old reverend would turn the town on its ear, if not lead it to righteousness.

Pa, I don't need to say, was not overly pleased with the idea. I overheard him complaining to Ma that he'd spent the better part of twelve years mopping up damage from the Reverend Pelham's sermons. Because, you see, it wasn't the wicked people who got changed by them. It wasn't even the pious and prim who were well set in their ways and not about to change, for all their tears and sweat. It was the meek and easily frightened—they who had a fragile hold on the everlasting mercy.

I felt terrible. I knew good and well it was the business of Mabel Cramm's bloomers that had set the congregation to thinking that the town was headed on the road to perdition. And me and Willie had done that just to get even with the Weston boys. It was like blowing a soap bubble to the size of a hot-air balloon. Even though God and I were on shaky terms in those days, I prayed He would see how the situation had got all out of proportion and stick a pin in it. Well, anyhow, that He would somehow manage to keep Reverend Pelham home in western Connecticut.

My prayer was not answered. Reverend Pelham wrote back the very day he got the letter. He said the Lord had told him to tear himself away from the sinners in Connecticut and hightail it to Leonardstown, where, apparently, the Devil had had a picnic since the reverend's departure twelve years before.

So it was that at eleven A.M. on the last Sunday morning in June the Reverend J. K. Pelham mounted the pulpit, standing where by all rights my pa should have been, breathing fire and brimstone on the just and unjust alike.

I wasn't too worried when he spoke out against drinking strong spirits and indulging in tobacco. I've never had anything more than a little hard cider myself, and the only thing I smoke regularly is corn silks and the occasional rabbit tobacco. In fact, I was wondering how Mr. Weston was taking that part of the sermon, since everyone knows he not only sells tobacco but is known to smoke and chew it himself. As for the strong drink, there were a number of menfolk out there that had regular bouts of indigestion for which alcoholic spirits had proved to be the only known cure. Or so they maintained.

I began to get a bit squirmy when he started in to preach about impure thoughts and language. How can you blame a fellow for what he thinks? It's not as if I go looking for ideas that aren't proper. Sometimes thoughts just pop into my head like weeds in the vegetable patch. The same goes for language. How can you blame a fellow for letting slip the occasional cuss word? I don't cuss around ladies or church members—only do it around Willie or other fellows. After I've had a run-in with the Weston boys, it takes a few purple phrases to settle me down.

Reverend Pelham did not stop with condemning folks for unrighteous behavior or even wicked thoughts and words. He went on to say that people who behave themselves might be in worse danger than the murderers, thieves, adulterers, and the like, because being good never got a soul past the Pearly Gates. No, no. We mustn't be misled. Behaving yourself didn't cut any ice with God if you didn't *believe* everything just exactly proper. When the Day of Judgment came, all us doubters and unbelievers and followers after false doctrine would come to the same end as all the outrageous sinners. We would all go swooping down the coal chute to the fiery furnace. No, those weren't his *exact* words, but that's what he meant.

If all this was not enough to scare the dead, the reverend took to hinting that we were not only panting to the end of the century, we were sneaking up on the End of the Age. Oh, yes, we might be sitting here fat and content, as it were, but we ought to be trimming our lamps like the wise virgins in the Bible. Although he admitted that the

Bible itself says, "No man knoweth the day or the hour," and he wasn't going to be presumptuous and name a particular day or hour. But when eighteen ninety-nine rolled over into nineteen aught aught, we'd be fools if we hadn't prepared ourselves for that Dread Day.

"There are those," he went on, and I swear he was looking straight at me when he did, "there are those sitting here in our very midst who will never sit at table in the Kingdom of Heaven. You know who you are!" He was staring daggers at me. "You know who you are." This second time he said it in a real sad way. "I beg you, my brother, turn from your evil thoughts. Turn again and be saved before the night cometh when no man can repent! Repent and join me on that glorious day in the Eternal Kingdom of the Righteous!"

Sitting there in the Leonardstown Congregational church, I just gave up trying to be a Christian. The whole business was too much of a burden for a fellow like me—high-tempered as I was and hating to be tamed down. Let's face it, I ain't got the knack for holiness. Besides, I didn't have the slightest little desire to join the likes of Reverend Pelham at the dinner table for fourteen minutes, much less at the banquet table of Heaven eternally. Eternity is a mighty long time to be stuck with people who judge every word you say and think and condemn most of what you do. It struck me as pretty miserable company. And if Reverend Pelham was the kind of company God preferred to keep, well, I just hoped they'd be happy together.

As for me, I would leave the fold and become either a heathen, a Unitarian, or a Democrat, whichever was most fun. Because if the reverend was by any chance in on God's secrets, the Dread Day (providing it was January first, nineteen aught aught) was only six months away. I aimed to pack a lot of living into that time, and Reverend Pelham had made it clear you couldn't do that and remain a faithful Congregationalist.

Reverend Pelham was, of course, eating at our house. The deacons thought it would be insulting, not to mention expensive, to put their beloved former pastor up in the Leonardstown Hotel.

Well, I got through Sunday dinner (during which the reverend pretty much repeated his earlier sermon, looking across the table to me as though he suspected I'd missed a word a two). As soon as I was excused from the table, I went off to find Willie. I'm not allowed to fish on Sundays, so we were lying on the side of the hill, staring at the clouds, chewing our wood-sorrel twigs, which taste, if you don't know it, almost like lemonade. I watched the sky for a while, listening to the song of a hermit thrush. When the bird hushed, I told Willie in a solemn voice that, as of that very morning, I was a convert to disbelief, and that since life threatened to be short, I was determined, as they say, to make hay while the sun still shone.

"But Robbie," Willie said, "if you don't believe in

God, how come you believe He's going to make the world end come January?"

I struggled for a logical answer. Willie's one fault is that he takes everything strictly literal. Not much imagination in him, for all his good qualities. "Wal, Willie," I started, moving my sorrel stick to the other side of my mouth, "it's like this. No man knows the day or hour, but you'd be a fool not to take precautions. Wouldn't I be mad if suddenly the end came and I hadn't made the most of my remaining days? Why, Willie, I tell you, I'd just be furious."

"You think deep, Robbie," he said, his voice fair dripping with respect.

"Thank you," I said modestly. "I reckon I do."

From far off down the valley echoed the whistle of the afternoon train coming up from the south. "I tell you one thing, Willie. If it all goes bust, I'm sure going to miss the trains."

"Don't God have any trains?"

"Think about it, Willie. If there is a Heaven, about which I am currently in grave doubt, everyone would have wings. You'd probably despise trains if you could fly. And then there'd be the problem of firing up the locomotive. If it's like the reverend says, the fire is all someplace else."

"Wal," he said, and quite cheerfully, too, "then you'd be more than likely to see a lot more trains than most, seeing how—"

"Just in case," I said, a bit hurriedly, "let's go down to the depot and see the train come in before we have to go home to supper."

We got there just in time. The locomotive was whooshing and blowing steam as it slowed down. It was only the clank of metal wheels on those silver rails that made us know it was a mighty invention of man and not a fire-breathing dragon of the old stories. We strained to see who was in the cab.

"It's Mr. Webb!" Willie yelled. I could hardly hear him over the noise of the engine. We both yelled as loudly as we could and waved like crazy. Mr. Webb waved back from the cab window, yelling something we couldn't understand. Mr. Webb is our favorite engineer. He's never too proud or too busy to wave at you.

We waited in respectful silence while one or two passengers climbed aboard. I sighed. I'd only ridden the train a couple of times, and then only as far as Tyler, which was just ten miles down the track. This train went on to Montreal in Canada, and from there you could catch a train that would take you west to Chicago and then another that would take you straight to California.

"Wal," I said, after the train pulled out and it was quiet again, "that's one thing."

"What is?"

"One thing I want to do before . . . you know. I want to ride a train so far west that it will drop into the Pacific Ocean if the brakes don't hold."

I could tell Willie didn't like the idea of dropping into the sea, but he didn't say so. "Won't you get homesick so far away from Vermont?"

"Nah," I said. "You know me, Willie. Do I strike you as the kind of feller who mopes around for his ma?"

"No," he said, "I guess not."

Later I remembered how he said it, and I wondered if he was remembering when his ma and pa died. He was only a little kid. He must have missed them something terrible.

You might think a fellow who'd given up believing in God would lose his appetite, but I didn't find this to be the case. Besides, Sunday night supper was nearly always flapjacks with maple syrup. I figured a boy who might have only a few months to live ought to eat up so as to have strength for all the adventures he was going to have to pile into them. Let's see. It was nearly the end of June. That was good. July Fourth always promised firecrackers and about as much excitement as a boy might want for a few days. Then I could begin to plan the rest of the summer. I wondered, considering the impending apocalypse, if school would open in September. I sighed. It probably would. Grownups would see to it—just in case our future was extended into the next century, after all.

Still, there was the summer, or most of it, wide open.

Even with flapjacks, supper was a sober meal. I know Pa says I am unfair and judge people too harshly, and maybe it's because I still want to blame Reverend Pelham for things that in truth were nobody's fault but mine. Nonetheless, I can't erase the memory of Reverend Pelham shoveling in those good griddlecakes while at the same time talking about how we had to set our minds on heavenly things. He wanted Pa to rejoice at how many people had truly repented after the morning service, and how he was just warming up, and how, after the evening message, the angels in Heaven would be singing alleluias because of all the sinners he'd dragged in. All right. He didn't say it exactly that way, but that was more or less the gist of it.

"More griddlecakes, Reverend Pelham?" Ma asked quietly.

"Don't mind if I do," he said.

I told Pa after supper that I had a terrible bellyache (I didn't want to break his heart and tell him I'd lost my faith) and didn't believe I could sit through the evening service. He stood there for a minute listening. Reverend Pelham was in the study with the door closed, but we could hear him pacing up and down practicing his sermon. Pa looked at me thoughtfully, felt my forehead, and said in a whisper, "I'm not feeling all that well myself, boy, but that doesn't mean either of us can stay home."

By the time he got up into the pulpit, I could have given Reverend Pelham's sermon for him. Besides, hadn't I decided not to believe in God anymore? Why did I need to listen at all? I spent that hour trying to figure out what

I wanted to do with the final days of my life.

Trains were high on the list, but getting to California by Christmas was about as likely as flying to the moon. Then I thought of something I had never done that would just break my heart if I never was able to do it in this life. I wanted once, just once, to ride in a motorcar. I even, just for a minute, imagined myself *driving* a motorcar, but that, like a train ride to California, seemed too far-fetched even for daydreaming. Riding in a motorcar would be enough. I began to make a picture in my mind of me riding in a motorcar, the wind blowing through my hair, horses shimmying off the road as I passed, people staring, their eyes full of envy and admiration.

Now, at that time I'd never actually seen a motorcar. I'd just read about them in the newspaper, where someone had done a drawing of one that was enough to make a boy's mouth water. Little did I imagine that motorcars were to play a large role in my future.

Reverend Pelham was to leave on the southbound morning train. I was rereading *Tom Sawyer*. I couldn't read it the day before because Mark Twain, like most of my favorite writers, is not thought suitable reading for a Sunday. I've tried to argue with Ma about this. "When does a person need comfort from a good book more than on a Sunday?" I asked. Beth just snorted. Seems all *her* favorite books are suitable for Sunday reading. What's happened to her? She used to like Mark Twain almost as much as I do. So I was in the kitchen reading fast and deep to make up for a whole day's deprivation, and I only half realized that Deacon Slaughter and Mr. Weston had come and were holed up with Pa and Reverend Pelham in Pa's study. The door was shut.

An hour or so later Ma hauled me out of my book in time to say good-bye to the reverend, which I did, being careful to use my best manners, so no one could tell how happy I was to be seeing the back of him.

The reverend thanked Ma very kindly for her gracious hospitality and good cooking and shook hands with all of us. He didn't even look funny when Elliot laughed and grabbed him by the left hand instead of the right.

Finally, he turned to Pa and said sort of sadly, "I will be praying for you, Brother Hewitt."

Pa was shaking his hand as he answered, "And I'll be praying for you, my friend."

Then Mr. Weston and Deacon Slaughter hustled the reverend out to Mr. Weston's buggy and off to the depot. I didn't know what all that praying back and forth meant until later that evening, when Ma sent me to the study to call Pa to supper. I opened the door and he was sitting there reading.

I guess I must have dropped my jaw to my knees for the pure shock. My pa was sitting right there in the manse of the Congregational church reading *The Descent of Man* by Mr. Charles Darwin. It was a well-known fact in Leonardstown that this book was inspired by the Devil himself.

Pa let me stare awhile before he said quietly, "J. K. Pelham is a good man, Robbie, but he appears to be afraid of new ideas. I don't believe God wants us to be afraid of ideas."

But the idea in that book, so Deacon Slaughter had announced one Wednesday night at prayer meeting, was that your great-great-great-great (and so forth) granddaddy was a monkey. I couldn't believe my pa, who was an ordained minister of the gospel and the father of impressionable children, would entertain such a horrifying notion. I said as much.

"I believe that God created us, Robbie, but I'm not wise enough to know just how he chose to do it. I think Mr. Darwin's theory merits study."

I couldn't understand. Pa was a preacher. He had no business reading heathen books that question the Bible. Also, how could he be so careless as to leave a terrible book like that just lying around where anyone could see it? No wonder Reverend Pelham was upset. As for Deacon Slaughter and Mr. Weston, they could tell the congregation not to hire Pa again when his year was up come next May. Then what would happen to us all? Pa didn't know any work but preaching. We'd all probably starve to death, if we didn't wind up on the poor farm. I was so upset, I left the room without telling him to come to supper, and Beth had to go fetch him.

• • •

The very next day, the first momentous event occurred. On Tuesday, June the twenty-seventh, 1899, at three P.M., I saw a motorcar. Pa had hired a surrey from the livery stable and was driving down to Tyler to see a parishioner. The man was a granite worker dying of the stonecutters' disease in the Tyler Sanatorium. "Want to go, Robbie?" he asked.

The fact that I'd lain awake half the night mad at him and worrying about what would become of us evaporated from my head like the dew of early morning. I even forgot I'd promised to go fishing with Willie. I couldn't imagine anything better than a trip to the city—except maybe a trip to the city with just me and Pa. As you've probably gathered by this time, to a preacher his family always comes last. First come the needy, then the parishioners, and then the family. And amongst the family I always felt that I got the short end.

I'm ashamed to keep complaining about Elliot, but the truth is he gets lots more attention than I ever do, maybe to make up for his twisted body and simple mind. Every year sets him more apart from boys his age. They're all big and braggy and thinking about girls. Elliot still plays with Letty. He's patient with her and lets her ride his crooked back and pull his hair like it's reins. He laughs when there's nothing to laugh at. It isn't to my credit that I have been a little bit ashamed over the years that he was the big brother and I was the younger. But still it used to cause me to pinch up inside—the attention that Pa gave to him. And he, of course, adores Pa. He kind of pants around him like a faithful dog. It used to embarrass me for folks to see a great big boy like that acting so simple—but my father always made it seem as though it was perfectly all right, as if he liked it, even.

So, between my brother and all the poor and needy of the village and the church folks who demand lots of chatting up and tending to from their minister, there's never been a lot of time left for me. Did Ma and the girls feel cheated? I don't know. I wasn't much worried about them. I was thinking mostly about myself those days.

So when Pa invited me to go to the city with him, I jumped at the chance. Besides, he had hired Nelly, who was my favorite horse in the livery stable. You'd think with a name like Nelly, she'd be as prim and set in her ways as a deacon's widow, but Nelly is about the jauntiest horse you could ever hope to see. When another horse pulls up alongside her, she's been known to break into a full gallop and keep it up most of the ten-mile road to Tyler. I was hoping something like that might occur, but it was a tame trip. Although Pa let me hold the reins most of the way, he wouldn't let me put her in a gallop on purpose. The excitement came after we hit the outskirts of Tyler.

There was such a hubbub at the town limits that Pa almost took the back road around to the sanatorium. Thank goodness he didn't. At first I didn't even recognize the thing. It just looked as though the crowd was milling about a carriage that had got unhitched. Then it hit me. The thing sitting right there on the main street of Tyler, Vermont, was a horseless carriage. I jumped out of the surrey. "I'll wait here!" I yelled to Pa.

The motorcar's wheels were big and spoked like buggy wheels. There was a high seat with a kind of lever. Someone said that was what you steered with. The motor was hidden. I think it was under the seat on which the driver sat. He was wearing a scarf and goggles and a huge overcoat even though it was hot enough to melt the tar in the sidewalks. He didn't smile much. I reckon when you own a motorcar, it doesn't do to look too casual. Every now and again when some grimy-fingered urchin would get too close, he'd raise an eyebrow and growl something like "Don't touch the finish. The Winton's just been polished," which seemed only right for such a grand man to say.

I kept hoping he would start the engine so I could see how it was done. I really wanted to hear the roar and see the motorcar blazing down the road, sending all the horses into a panic. But he just sat there in the center of that curious and mostly awestruck crowd. Now and again someone would ask a question like, "How fast does it go really?" or taunt him, saying, "Bet you couldn't keep up with my horse." The driver would look superior—as well he might, owning such a beauty—and remark off-hand that he wouldn't put it in a race with a horse, hinting by his manner that it would be cruel to get the poor beast in such a lather. Why, the poor critter might drop dead from exhaustion.

Pa came back far too soon, even though he had been gone fully an hour by the clock on the Unitarian church steeple. I tried to persuade him to wait a bit, hoping maybe the man would start the motorcar and we could actually see it run, but he just laughed. "It doesn't look as if that fellow is going to move until those gawkers head for home, and that may be suppertime. We've got to get the horse and buggy back to Jake's before then."

From that day on, my ambition was fixed. I was determined. Someday, if the world didn't end before I grew up and got rich, I was going to own a motorcar. And if six months was all I had left, I was at any rate determined to have a ride in one before the world went bust.

There was a problem, however. No one in Leonardstown owned a motorcar. How could I ride in one if no one I knew had one? To my knowledge, and I knew pretty near everything that went on in our village, no motorcar had ever even come through Leonardstown.

I consulted Willie the next morning when we went on our delayed fishing trip. He wasn't very happy with me going off to the city without letting him know *and* seeing a motorcar when he wasn't around. I tried to cheer him up, saying that when I owned one, I would give him a ride whenever he wanted.

"If the world comes to an end this year, there's not much chance you're ever going to own one," he grumped.

33

"Exactly what I was thinking, Willie. So my best bet is to get to ride in one sometime in the next six months."

"You ain't seen but one motorcar since you was born more than ten years ago. How come you're not only going to *see* another one in six months, but you're going to go *riding* in it to boot? Don't seem likely to me."

"Just what I was thinking, Willie. But there's got to be a way. I just got to have that one satisfaction before the end comes."

"Too bad you can't pray."

"What do you mean?"

"Well, when I want something impossible, I ask God for it because God can do the impossible. But you can't pray."

"Why not? My father's the preacher. I'm a ten times better pray-er than you are."

"You don't believe in God no more. Remember?"

"Well, I could pray just in case."

"I don't think it would work. God would know."

I ignored Willie and that evening slipped in a to-whom-it-may-concern prayer to say that before the world collapsed in dust and ashes, I would sure like to ride in a motorcar just once.

3
The Glorious Fourth

We always get excited about the Fourth of July. Why wouldn't we? It is the biggest thing ever to happen in our town, if you don't count the ice storm that broke down half the trees and let us ice-skate down Main Street on Christmas Day a few years back. But that only happened once. Fourth of July happens every year.

We love the parade. First comes the marshal, who also happens to be the mayor, and since we've had the same mayor all my life, it's always been Mr. Earl Weston. Mr. Weston is the mayor because no one else can spare the time. I don't mean that only lazy men go into politics, but Earl Weston has some mysterious source of money that means he doesn't have to farm, or work in the quarries or stone sheds, or slog away in the livery stable or blacksmith shop, or preach like my pa. He doesn't even clerk in his own store. He was the one, I understand, who thought a board of selectmen wasn't a fancy-enough government for a growing town on the main line of the railroad and that we ought to have a mayor. When no one

35

else could understand why, he volunteered. I reckon Mr. Weston figured out that somebody has to lead off the Fourth of July parade, and that it was only fitting that that someone be the town's mayor. If anybody grumbled, I never heard tell of it.

So first comes the mayor. He is riding, of course. Up until that time Mr. Earl Weston had not been known to walk far, and since he owns his own buggy, he might as well ride in it. Then, mostly walking, come the veterans. Now, the Civil War was over in 1865, and this is 1899, so only the ones who went as youngsters are near spry anymore, and some of them is downright decrepit. But they are mostly walking behind Mr. Weston's buggy, except for Colonel Weathersby, who is a farmer and owns his own horse and thinks that a colonel should ride a horse if he's got one handy. And all of us boys agree. Colonel Weathersby's horse is a beautiful Morgan. He's black and sleek and adds a lot of class to the parade. The veterans need the dignity of that horse, because they are by and large shuffling along. Rafe Morrison lost an arm, and so he's got this empty sleeve sewed up, and Warren Smith is still on crutches on account of a missing leg, but he insists on walking the whole route even so. I think he's kind of thumbing his nose at Mr. Earl Weston, but I ain't heard anyone else say as much, so I keep it to myself.

We got twenty-seven veterans in our town, but only about nineteen or twenty were in the parade. The other citizens that went to the Civil War are sleeping in the cemetery up on East Hill or in some cornfield grave down south.

This year there are two men returned from the war in Cuba, but neither of them got farther away than Tennessee. They are walking toward the back of the parade so as not to draw attention away from the real veterans of the Grand Army of the Republic.

The town band follows the veterans. We got a pretty good band for a town our size. This is on account of Mr. Pearson, who used to teach music at the military college in Northfield and then retired to his old family farm right outside town. He heard our band once and volunteered the next day to take it over. Believe me, he whipped it into shape, and now our band is the pride and envy of the whole county. Someday I'm going to get ahold of a cornet and play in the band, if I can just figure out how to get one. As I was listening to the band, wishing for a cornet, I caught myself hoping all over again that the world wouldn't come to an end. It would wreck all my plans for the future.

So there's the band, sixteen strong including a big bass drum that makes you jump like a bullfrog if Owen Higgins happens to boom it just as he passes you. But this past July I wasn't standing on the sidelines. Me and Willie decorated his old wagon, and we were marching in the parade. We meant to pull his aunt Millie's cat in the wagon, but every time we practiced, the cat would just jump out and run away.

"What about your little sister?" Willie asked. "I bet

she'd sit there proper. Your ma could dress her in red, white, and blue." I was horrified. Letty was only five years old. I never got to be in the parade when I was five years old. It didn't seem fitting somehow. But the trouble was, Willie mentioned it to Letty before I made up my mind, and she went running to Ma, and so we were stuck with pulling my baby sister in the wagon.

You may be surprised to know that it ain't easy pulling a little girl the whole length of a parade in a wagon. No, she didn't try to jump out or anything. She was pleased as punch just to sit there. But Willie thought as soon as he'd pulled a few feet that since she was my sister I should have the honor. I soon saw why. That little scallywag was heavy. I was sweating like a plow horse. And the wheels were funny, so no matter how straight I pulled, the wagon kept moving to the left.

First thing I knew, I had hit Ned Weston's brand-new bicycle. The Weston boys are very particular about their precious wheels, and Ned claimed right out loud that I was jealous and did it on purpose. Now, you're obliged to belt someone for an insult of that magnitude, parade or no parade. Willie caught my fist in midair. "People is watching!" he muttered, so I had to give up fighting for the time being and endure another of Ned's superior smirks.

Even including that unfortunate incident, it was a jim-dandy of a parade. The Ladies' Society of the Methodist church (they aren't as dignified as the Congregational ladies) had this farm wagon with streamers on it, and the ladies were standing and sitting around all decked out in flowers. I forget what the banner read—"The Methodist Ladies are the Flower of Vermont Womanhood" or some such. The Congregational ladies smiled politely from the sidelines, but you could tell they were a little bit miffed.

The Grange had a wagon, too. July is too early to show off much in the way of the fruit of the land, but they had a few unhappy lambs and heifers on board to baa and bleat and represent the glory of our agricultural tradition. Rachel Martin and some of the other girls were riding in that one. They were smiling bravely, though you had the feeling that, standing there in the middle of all that live-stock, they'd rather be pinching their noses.

There was a wagon of stonecutters, mostly just the Scotch and French-Canadian ones. The Italian stonecut-ters stood on the sidelines, looking on and laughing. I think personally that some of their jollity came from a bottle of that homemade wine, which as you know is ille-gal, unlike cider, which may serve the same effect when it gets a little elderly but is a Vermont product and therefore perfectly legal and not frowned down upon. Pa says judg-mentalism is one of my worst failings, next to my temper, and besides, spirits is spirits, and at least the Italians are honest about their drinking habits. Pa always takes up for the Italian stonecutters. He says they're not just stone-cutters, they're sculptors in the tradition of Michelangelo and the only true artists we got around here.

This year the Wilson children were riding ponies. They are younger than me, but their rich grandpa gave them each a pony. Another of my failings, you might as well know, is the sin of envy. And to tell the truth, I was more jealous of those ponies than I was of Tom and Ned Weston's new sets of wheels. But since it was plain impossible to imagine ever owning a pony, I spent most of my sin of covetousness that day on the Weston boys' wheels, because owning a bicycle seemed closer to possible than owning a pony. No point in wasting a sin on something that's just plain not going to happen in this world. I kept forgetting that I had decided not to believe in God and that therefore it didn't matter about sin anymore. Old habits die hard, as my grandma used to say.

It was a good parade while it lasted, but once it was done, Willie and I dragged Letty home as fast as her weight and those wobbly wheels would allow. It was nearly noon, but I begged off dinner, as did Willie. Ma made us sandwiches to take to the creek. She didn't have to tell us to be home before dark. There would be fireworks at dark, and besides, supper would come before that. A couple of sandwiches apiece would not suffice to stave off starvation between morning and bedtime.

Wouldn't you know? Fast as we hurried, Ned and his big brother Tom was sitting sassy as overfed cats at Willie's and my fishing spot. Ned knew perfectly well whose spot it was. He had seen Willie and me there often enough. I wanted like Christmas to teach him the lesson I hadn't been able to earlier that morning, but his brother Tom is two years older than me and a good boxer to boot, so I decided that it was one of those occasions when "digression is the better part of valor," and me and Willie had to be content with our second-favorite spot.

We were quiet for a long time, busying ourselves threading our worms on our hooks, making a few trial throws, until finally we settled back into the bank, our caps over our eyes to shade them from the sun. I sighed. With the heat and the loss of our best place, we weren't liable to need many worms.

"So," said Willie after a while, "you still an apeist, Robbie?"

"A what?"

"You know," he said in a dignified tone, "one of them there heathens who don't believe in God."

I hadn't known the proper term for people like me, and it was months before I found out that the word was *atheist,* not *apeist.* When Willie said "apeist," my first impulse was to thump him on the head. But I controlled myself. Maybe it was all in one package, and if I was going to be an unbeliever, I had to be an apeist whether I liked the notion of monkey granddaddies or not. Besides, I pride myself on having the largest vocabulary in Leonardstown school, on account of all the reading I do. I couldn't admit to not knowing the proper word for what I had determined to become. "I reckon," I said, even

41

though the monkey part made me queasy in the belly. "Eh-yup. One of them apeists."

"Ain't you—wal, ain't you the least bit scared?"

"Scared of what?" I probably sounded belligerent.

"I mean, apeists is liable to end up going someplace you wouldn't be all that pleased to end up in."

"You forget, Willie," I said, as much to myself as to him, "if there ain't no God, there ain't no down nor up."

He considered this for a minute or two, twitching his line a bit. "Neither one, eh?" he asked at last.

"Stands to reason, don't it?"

"I reckon."

"I forget sometimes," I confessed, to soften it some. "I forget that I don't believe anymore. I been known to throw up a prayer now and again."

"Yeah?"

"It don't do no good nor harm neither, I suppose." I jerked my pole up and threw the line farther out. Not a nibble. Curse those blinking Westons. "But it is a relief," I continued, "not to have to bother myself anymore about commandments."

He sat straight up. "What are you talking about?"

"You see, Willie"—I felt just like Pa must when he's trying to explain the Bible to thick-headed parish-ioners—"it stands to reason, don't it? If a person don't believe in God, then he don't have to worry about all that stuff in the Bible anymore. Why, just now I was sitting here thinking I wanted to cuss those durned Westons for taking our best hole. So I just went right ahead and helped myself. I can cuss anytime I feel like it now. The commandments don't apply."

"The *Ten* Commandments?"

What other commandments were there? "Sure," I said. "If I need to lie or steal or cuss or"—and here I felt a little shiver go through me as I said it—"or do somebody in . . ."

Willie was up on his feet staring down at me like I'd suddenly turned into a porcupine.

"Or be wicked on Sunday or commit 'dultry—"

"Hush your mouth, Robbie Hewitt. Suppose your father heard you talking this way."

"I would never tell him," I said grandly. "It would break the poor man's heart."

Willie sat down again, still considering what his best friend had become. Finally he lay back against the bank. "You better think this through careful, Robbie," he said quietly.

"You think I ain't give it proper thought?" I said. "Why, it's practically all I think about anymore." Which was not true. I thought an awful lot about motorcars and bicycles. (Was there any chance of my ever owning a pair of wheels?) And would the members want to throw Pa out after the next annual meeting of the congregation because he wasn't thrilled enough about eternal damnation? I—though I could hardly confess it even to myself, much less to Willie—I even thought about Rachel

Martin, who sat right in front of me at school—how it might feel to give one of those corkscrew curls of hers a proper yank, just to see if it boinged back in place like a pond frog. But faced as I was with the end of the world, it didn't seem fitting to have thoughts about girls with dark brown curls hanging down their backs. Anyhow, thoughts of Rachel Martin made me a little itchy under the collar, even when I never breathed them out loud.

We were quiet a long time, lying against the bank, chewing our wood-sorrel sticks, our lines only moving with the gentle current, the smell of the new-mown fields in our noses, the hum of insects in our ears. At the time it seemed the Fourth of July would last forever. But there was a sadness already in the lazy call of a crow, as if it knew that everything was all downhill from here, like it was the beginning of the end of our last summer on earth.

"So," said Willie, and when he did, I realized that he had said it more than once and I hadn't been paying attention. "So, what do you want to do?"

At that moment I didn't want to do anything but lie against the bank of the North Branch and get mildly drunk on the smells of midsummer and listen to the stream laughing past and the insects busy humming in my ears. I didn't answer. Willie didn't ask again. I think he was content, too. It had been a great parade, even with having to pull that bum wagon with Letty aboard.

I allowed myself the luxury of a daydream of next summer's parade. Me on a pair of wheels from W. R.

Nichols in Tyler. The ad in the Tyler paper was framed in a double-thick black-lined box. I had the words memorized: "Bicycles, the most complete of any in the city and I will sell them at any price you want!"

That was a lie, of course, because the ad went right on to say the price Mr. Nichols wanted.

"Prices from $20 to $125," which was sure not any price *I* wanted, my total savings at the moment being a whopping $1.35. But there was this tantalizing phrase at the bottom of the lying ad: "A large number of second-hand wheels almost given away in the basement of the Nichols Block. Come and see me!"

All right, it sounded a little bit like the witch in "Hansel and Gretel" inviting the young folks into her gingerbread house, but I could hardly resist walking the ten miles to Tyler to find out. What did "almost given away" mean, exactly? A dollar thirty-five? That would certainly be a giveaway compared to $20 or $125. Just who on God's green earth would pay $125 for a pair of wheels? Boy, if I had $125, I wouldn't waste it on any fancy bicycle. I'd go straight out and buy me a Winton motorcar like the one I saw in Tyler. I sighed. No, motorcars probably cost a fortune, more like a thousand dollars than a hundred.

Missing Elliot

No fish that afternoon—too hot and the wrong spot—but supper made up for it. We hadn't had as good a meal since the Reverend Pelham left town. Ma roasted up one of the older chickens that had given up laying. It was hardly tough at all the way she did it. On top of chicken we had baked beans and Indian pudding and some kind of custard.

Pa was very jolly and talked about the parade. He even spoke kindly of how good me and Willie had been pulling Letty the whole length of the parade route. I guess he hadn't heard about my little alteration with Ned Weston. At least he never mentioned it. He and Ma had stayed for all the speeches on the town hall green. Mr. Weston had surprised everyone by only speaking an hour and a half—a full forty minutes short of his previous record.

As good as supper was, we hurried it a bit. The band concert was due to begin at six-thirty, while it was still light, and we didn't want to miss any of it. And yes, Letty could stay up for the fireworks. Both Beth and I were obliged to object. We'd never been allowed to stay up that late when we were five, but it was a halfhearted protest. We were all in too good a mood. Besides, if Letty was put to bed, one of us might be recruited to stay home with her. We couldn't take that chance.

By quarter past six we had a blanket spread out on the green. We're a big family for one blanket, so we had to sit close together. I huddled against Pa. "You cold, Robbie?" he asked. I nodded yes, so he put his arm around me. I wasn't really cold, but somehow I was feeling that if I got more than an inch away from the warmth of his big body, I was likely to freeze. Was that what being out on your own in the cold, cruel world meant? Was it like the coldness you feel on a summer night when you can't get close enough to your pa's big, warm presence?

It didn't last. Letty keeled over, dead asleep, and Pa reached out and picked her up and held her, cradling her head against his chest. She didn't even wake up when the band started tuning up, just kind of stirred a bit and settled down.

"I guess I'll go sit with Willie," I said.

"All right," Pa said, smiling. I wanted him to say something like "Don't go. Sit here with us," but he didn't.

I would have really enjoyed the band concert except I couldn't get over how cold it was—though it was July the Fourth and not dark yet. But then the concert ended and the fireworks were on. It's hard to think about much else when the sky is exploding: rockets whizzing and whining and blasting to great umbrellas of shattered light all over the town and as far as the mountains on either side. I wondered, but not in a scary way, mind you, just wondered if the end of the world could hold a candle to those fireworks for aerial excitement.

"Robbie, have you seen Elliot?" I jumped up at the sound of Pa's voice. He had startled me there in the dark, my mind being on the convulsions of light in the sky. He was standing behind me, a kerosene lantern in one hand.

"No, Pa, no I ain't." I could tell he was worried when he didn't correct my grammar.

"You boys help me look for him?"

"Sure, Mr. Hewitt." Willie was on his feet now, tucking his shirttail into his pants, all business.

"Sit down and be quiet," somebody said loudly and rudely from a few feet behind us, so we moved off, Willie folding his blanket as we headed off the green and into Main Street.

"We were all here together watching the display when he said he had to go—I was afraid he might—well, I had Letty on my lap, so I just told him to run along home and use the privy there. He didn't come back right away. At first I didn't worry, but then—well, he was gone so long, I went home to see what the trouble was, and he's nowhere around. I—I can't locate him."

"Don't worry, Mr. Hewitt." Willie sounded like somebody's mother. "We'll find him, sure."

Pa smiled a sort of crooked thank-you. He held out the lantern. "Here, you boys take this. I can manage."

I took the lantern from him, not knowing what else to do. It was a dark night except when an exceptionally large display lit the sky momentarily. "Where should we look?" I asked, half scared about Elliot and half grumpy to be pulled away from the fireworks.

"I'm thinking I'd better head up toward the quarry," Pa said. "God forbid—"

I jammed the lantern handle back into his hand. "You take the light, then," I said.

"Yeah," said Willie. "You'll need it worse than us. Anyhow, I can get one when we pass my house. We'll look around the crowd. He's likely ran into a pal and is just setting here watching the show." You could tell how hard Willie was trying to buck Pa up. He knew good and well Elliot didn't have any pals except maybe his friend Jesus.

"Perhaps . . ." Pa said. "But it probably makes sense to look around here first. Thank you, boys." With that he hurried off in the direction of East Hill Road—the one that passes the cemetery and ends up at the quarry, which is about a fifty-foot-deep hole in the ground lined with nothing but granite rock. I shivered, as both Willie and me watched until the dark swallowed Pa up.

"Where you think Elliot is?" Willie asked.

"How should I know?" I snapped. It was hard enough having a brother like Elliot without having him disappear in the middle of the Fourth of July fireworks,

49

worrying your pa half to distraction.

We looked around the crowd as best we could, but people didn't take kindly to us peering down at their blankets. Soon Willie said, "Let's go home and get another lantern. Then we can see what we're doing."

We headed toward Willie's house. His aunt was already asleep. Fireworks or no fireworks, the woman kept absolutely regular hours. Willie and me tried hard to tiptoe and whisper, but before we were three feet inside the door, I stumped my toe on the cat's water dish, sending it clanking across the wood floor.

"Who's there?!"

"Just us, Aunt Millie."

"Why aren't you in bed, William?"

"Me and Robbie got to help Reverend Hewitt look for Elliot. He kinda wandered away during the fireworks. I come to fetch a lantern."

She mumbled something from her room down the hall, which we took as permission. Willie got the lantern from the pantry. He waited until we were safely outside to strike the match and light it. The sudden sulfur smell of the lucifer match brought to mind Reverend Pelham's spare-no-details description of Hell. I shook myself to be rid of such a thought.

We tried to think of all of Elliot's favorite places, the general store being top of the list because that's where all the candy is. There was no one near the darkened storefront. No Elliot peering into the front glass window or sitting on the edge of the porch, swinging his legs. We went back to the fireworks just to make sure he hadn't returned, but they were over and the crowd was breaking up. People started to wander down the street in both directions, heading home.

"Should we find your ma?"

I shook my head. "She'd only worry," I said.

We tried the livery stable next. Only old Rube Wiley was around, but he hadn't seen "head nor hair of no one with less than four legs" since the concert began hours before. "I'd help you look, boys, but all that banging has made these horses skittery as brides the day before the wedding."

We walked to the south end of Main. Then we circled behind the houses on the west side, next behind the houses on the east side. We checked the green once more to make sure Elliot hadn't somehow returned. All we found was a blanket and a wicker basket that someone would be hunting for come morning.

"Better try the railroad tracks—and the creek," Willie said.

Lord have mercy. Surely Elliot wouldn't go to the creek in the middle of the night. Surely he had more sense than that! I followed Willie back up Main and then down Depot Street. We swung the lantern around the platform and down the tracks. Then we crossed them, recrossed Main, and walked along the North Branch at least half a mile.

"He wouldn't have headed for the pond, would he?"

"Nah! He ain't a total idiot!" I was talking too loud, trying to outyell the thought of Elliot floating facedown in the middle of Cutter's Pond.

"C'mon, Robbie. Nobody's calling nobody nothing. I'm just trying to think of everything."

"I know," I said. "Let's go check around the stone sheds. If he ain't there, we'd best go home. Why, he's probably there right now, safe and sound, while you and me is running around looking for him like crazy men."

There was no sign of him around the stone sheds, their low metal roofs gleaming ghostly under the single tall gaslight. It didn't help to know that under those roofs lay hundreds of gravestones in the making. We headed up West Hill Road, then turned at School Street, not talking until we reached the manse. Neither Elliot nor Pa was there, but Ma was so relieved to see Willie and me that she refused to let me go out again. "Go on home, Willie. Your aunt will be frantic if you stay out much longer. Mr. Hewitt will find Elliot. I know he will. Thank you, though." She gave him a large piece of pie to eat on the way and hurried him out the door.

Letty was already in bed. Ma and Beth and I sat at the table and tried not to look at each other's faces, pale and drawn in the gaslight of the kitchen.

"He's dead. I just know he's dead," Beth burst out.

"Oh, Beth, I'm sure he's all right." But how could Ma be so sure?

The silence among us was so huge that each tick of

the hall clock hit my head like the stroke of Teacher's ruler against my palm. I cleared my throat.

"What, Robbie?" Ma looked at me all expectant, as though I might have come up with a good idea. I felt pushed to say something.

"Me and Willie combed the town—all Elliot's favorite spots. We even hunted up the creek." The look of fear that crossed her face made me hurry on. "It's running low," I said. "You know how dry it's been."

She tried to smile.

Beth scraped back her chair and got noisily to her feet. "I can't stand just sitting here staring," she said.

Ma looked up, all lit up with hope. She really thought one of us was going to come up with some great idea, but we didn't have any, not any we could bear to put into words. The quarries east of town and the pond to the south—they were too unthinkable.

I made a picture in my mind of Pa, the lantern swinging in his right hand, climbing East Hill Road toward Quarry Hill. He was calling out, *Elliot! Elliot!* and then a little voice from the dark calls back, *Here I am, Pa.* And he takes Elliot by his big left hand and brings him home, rejoicing.

"I'll make some tea," Beth said, bringing me back to reality.

"Thank you, Beth," Ma said, her voice low with disappointment. "That would be nice."

We drank our tea. I put two large lumps of maple

sugar into mine, stirred it as hard as if it was porridge, blew across it, and slurped it. Nobody corrected me, not even Beth. I wished they would.

At first we couldn't be sure. When you been listening for what seems like hours, your ears strained with the waiting and wanting to hear the sound that's not there, you hardly dare to trust them when it does come. Then, suddenly, we all jumped up at once and ran to the door. Our chairs clattered backwards to the floor, but we didn't stop to right them. Ma got there first and yanked the door wide.

There was Pa, bent nearly in half with the effort of carrying a long load of what we knew was Elliot onto the porch. Ma gave a sharp cry and was still. None of us could breathe.

"He's all right," Pa said quietly, answering the question we couldn't bear to voice. "Just very, very tired." He came on into the kitchen and gently laid Elliot's crooked frame down on the daybed we keep in there in case someone is sick and needs to stay close to the stove. Slowly Pa straightened up and kind of crunched his shoulders. "He was in the cemetery. I found him stumbling around the tombstones. He didn't seem to know why he'd gone up there. I asked him, but he couldn't seem to explain." He turned toward Ma. "It doesn't matter, does it? He's safe."

"Oh, Frederick," Ma said. "Thank God."

He kept looking at her for a minute, and then he went over to the door where she was still standing and, right in front of us children, he put his arms around her, laid his head on top of hers, and commenced to weep.

"I went all the way to the quarry. . . . It was too dark to see anything down in the . . . in the . . . I was so afraid . . ." The words were coming out between the sobs. I may not have heard them just right, but I swear that is what it sounded like he said.

I shut my eyes. I wanted to clap my hands over my ears as well. How could I bear to witness it? My pa hanging on to Ma, crying like a baby. It did something to the pit of my belly. I was ashamed for him. Even when he humiliated me or carried on against war, I'd never seen him when he was anything less than a real man. But at that moment he was not the tall preacher that folks had to crane their necks to look up to, not only physically but in every way. He was a scared little boy. It was all I could do to keep from running out of the room.

"It's all right now, Frederick. It's all over now." Ma was patting his back and comforting him like he was Letty and not her husband. "It's all right."

Finally, Pa let her go and reached into his pocket for his handkerchief and blew his nose. He laughed in a funny, choked kind of way. "My," he said, "you'd think I was the lost one."

He blew his nose once more before pocketing his handkerchief and going over to the daybed. He bent nearly double to get his head as close to Elliot's as he could. "How're we doing, young man?" he asked softly.

"It's aw right, Pa," Elliot whispered back. "I wa' scare', too."

"Good thing we found each other then, eh, son?" His voice was so gentle, so full of love that at that moment I was seized with such a jealousy of Elliot that if I had been abiding by the commandments, I would have shattered the one on covetousness to powdered smithereens. How could Pa love Elliot that much? Elliot wasn't a son a man could take pride in. He was a poor simpleton to be pitied. He'd never grow up and accomplish anything in this world. Mercy. He'd never even be able to shoulder the duties of the stupidest farmhand or stableboy. Pa and Ma were likely to be taking care of him the rest of their natural lives, and then who'd have the burden of him? No one in his right mind would want it. But here was Pa worshipping his poor simple boy like a wise man come to the manger. Whatever else it all meant, I knew better than I knew my own name that I had never heard Pa speak to me in such a voice. He'd never cried for me.

Nobody was paying me the least attention, so I climbed on upstairs to my room—to Elliot's and my room—and went to bed. I couldn't sleep. I kept hearing the sound of Pa's crying in my head. At long last I heard his heavy footsteps on the stairs. He was carrying Elliot to his own bed.

"Night, Robbie," he said. "Thanks for helping."

I turned my face to the wall and pretended to be asleep.

5
Disturbing Revelations

I was up nearly with the roosters the next morning, up before anybody except Ma. Sometimes I wondered if she ever slept. There she was, the fire stoked up, stirring the porridge. It was the same Scots blood in her that had caused her to name me Robert Burns Hewitt that made her boil that porridge, summer or winter.

I didn't feel hungry, but I knew it made no difference to say so. I wouldn't get out of the house until I'd downed my bowl of it. It's not that bad, porridge isn't, but it's heavy and sticky, and if you don't happen to be hungry, it's like wading waist deep through a bog.

Ma watched while I poured about twice the usual amount of maple syrup on it, but she didn't object. She just stood there, her lips parted a little ways, no words coming out. She looked dog tired. In a way I was ashamed of behaving in what I knew was a defiant manner, taking all that syrup, but I needed it that morning—needed sweetening, I reckon, or just some kind of proof that I was worth something extra to her, if not to Pa.

"You're up early, Robbie," she said, turning back to the big iron stove that takes up a quarter of the back wall.

"Yes, ma'am," I said. "Couldn't sleep too good."

"I guess it was a hard night for us all," she said. "But it's all right now. Elliot's safe and sound."

"Yes, ma'am." I chewed my way through another bite. Mercy, it was work to get through a whole bowl of porridge. I asked for another mug of milk. I needed help to wash it down. I stretched across the wide table to hand her the empty mug.

"I'm glad to see it hasn't hurt your appetite," she said, refilling my mug. Instead of reaching across, she walked around the table to give it to me.

I grunted, but she took it for a thank-you and patted my shoulder when she put the milk down at my place. Then she went to the stove, poured herself a cup of tea, and sat down at the table opposite me. Ordinarily I would have been pleased. She hardly ever took the time to sit down like that just with me. She bent her head over her cup and took a tiny sip. Then she sat back and stared into the space above my head.

It relieved me that she wasn't going to try to make conversation. I wasn't feeling chatty, and I still had half a bowl of porridge to work my way through.

"Your father's sleeping like a baby," she said finally. "I've never seen him so exhausted."

I nodded and swallowed and washed down what was

still stuck in my throat. She sighed deeply and took another sip of her tea.

I took her distraction as a chance to escape. I got up and hastily washed out my half-finished bowl under the kitchen tap. "Wal," I said in a fake cheery voice, "I guess me and Willie will try some fishing before the day gets too hot."

She nodded and smiled absentmindedly. She'd quite forgotten to ask me if I had finished all my porridge. I hightailed it out of there as fast as I could grab my pole and basket and jump off the porch.

Just as luck would have it, Willie's aunt had him splitting wood for the cookstove. "You found Elliot okay, I guess," he said as I came near.

I shrugged a yes. "Wanna go fishing?"

"I ain't ate yet," he said, studying my face.

"Come when you can," I said. "Maybe I'll go up and check the cabin first anyhow."

"The cabin?" We always went up to our hideout together. We both knew that. "You okay, Robbie?"

"I don't know, Willie. I just need to mess around a little. See if everything's all right, dig a few worms up there in the woods." I tried to sound ordinary. "I'll get back down to the creek before the Weston boys think about getting up. Promise."

"All right, then. See you." He brought the ax down dead in the center of the log. The boy can sure split wood. You got to give him credit for that.

I started for the hill directly from Willie's, skirting the field where the Robertses had their bull penned, crossed their pasture, and headed toward the edge of the woods from there. It wasn't the best way to get to the cabin. It would have been easier to go back down School Street and go up from my house, but I didn't want Pa or anyone to see me. I really needed to be by myself, even though I wasn't finding myself particularly delightful company just then. I wished I'd brought a book to read, but for that I'd have to go back home. I wasn't going back home until hunger drove me to it.

The hay on the hill had been mowed just a few days before, and the stubble was prickly but not overly painful. If I have a good quality, in addition to my prodigious vocabulary, it is my feet. They are as tough as hippo hide. I can't help being proud of them. I bet I could walk on nails like those swamis in India should the necessity arise. When I hit the first line of trees, I walked along parallel to the woods until I could look far down the hill to the back of Mabel Cramm's house—she who started it all—then down to the Branscoms', the Wilsons', and, of course, the Websters' farmhouse, barn, and chicken yard. All the fields and pastures behind School Street belonged to them. Then there was the big, rambling manse, and below that the steeple of the Congregational church pointing upward to the empty sky. I sighed. It seemed lonely to be an apeist that morning.

I didn't spot any tiny figures outside the manse.

Nobody splitting wood. There's never any need to split wood before breakfast at our house. Pa makes sure the wood box is full at all times. He's really faithful about that.

Sometimes, if people are out of work or needing help, he'll hire them to chop or split wood, but mostly he does it himself. "Get Robbie to give you a hand with that," Ma will say, but he'll just smile and shrug. "It's good for me," he'll say. I can't help but notice that whenever there's some little upset in the congregation, wood is just overflowing that box to the floor beside it, and the wood-pile outdoors is taller than me.

I turned and put the morning sun, now high in the sky and drifting southward, at my back and entered the woods. Suddenly my world was dark and cool. Since the snow melted, Willie and I had worn the path down until it was nearly as smooth as Main Street. I don't know why we went to the cabin so much. Oh, we kept a little stuff there—some extra fishing gear, a couple of old shirts for warmth in a cold snap, some lucifer matches to make fires, a couple of homemade cob pipes, and some corn silks we'd dried in case we needed a smoke. From time to time we'd try to store a little food—green apples we'd pinched from the Websters' orchard, some butter-nuts we were planning to eat as soon as we took the trouble to smash them open. Mostly the squirrels and coons got into the food. I was always surprised, when I went up, if they'd left anything for us.

In the quiet of the woods the sound came into my head as clear as if I was really hearing it. The sound of Pa crying. It was so unlike him. I think that was what turned me inside out. So unmanly. Whatever some folks may think about preachers who work more with their heads than their hands, nobody ever accused my pa of being anything less than a real man.

All because of Elliot. Because he was lost and might not have been found safe and then was. I've tried all my life not to mind Elliot being my brother, not to let him spoil what is, by and large, a pretty good life for a boy. Once the Weston boys talked about him just loud enough to make sure I could hear them, wondering whether Elliot's "condition" was a family weakness or a family sin. I gave Ned Weston a bloody nose for that one. To me it was a questioning of my parents' honor. I couldn't let that pass. I'm proud to say that even when Tom got big enough to whip me, the Westons didn't hold that discussion in my hearing again.

When I was younger, Ma and Pa would sometimes urge me to play with Elliot. "You used to have such good times together," they'd say, hoping I'd remember how when I was a toddler I loved romping with Elliot. But by the time I was four, I didn't want to play with Elliot anymore. He was big and clumsy. He knocked over all my block towers and broke my toy boats. As I grew older, I passed him by in the race of life. We couldn't talk about books, because when I was devouring Robert Louis

Stevenson, he couldn't even read the first primer. He could never catch any ball I threw him, and he was hopeless with a bat. Baseball only made him cry in frustration. If we walked down to the pond to swim, he was too slow to keep up. Nor could he get the hang of swimming, so if he went with me, I had to stay in the shallow water every minute for fear he'd wander out above his head and drown.

Usually he stayed home with Beth and Ma. Beth always liked Elliot better than me. I was too independent for her tastes. He worshipped her, trailed her around, and obeyed her. He loved the paper dolls she made for him and played with them by the hour. He never in his life sassed her or wished to heaven she'd never been born first.

Letty, when she came along, fit right in with the two of them. They made a great pet of her, and she adored them both. Sometimes Ma would rope me in to watch Letty, but usually I could slip out of the noose. I was the freest member of the family.

It's hard to see the cabin from any distance away. It has sort of folded itself into its surroundings. Only the chimney half is still upright. It's like a great toadstool with a chimney attached, which some giant has come along and stomped, crushing one end. I sometimes wonder if the smashed-in part of the roof might not just come crashing down on us someday, but I guess I'm not too worried about it, or I would have quit going there a long time ago.

I never fail to wonder what became of those folks who built our cabin. It dates back to the days when Revolutionary War veterans who had passed through this beautiful Vermont wilderness during the war came back, bringing their families up from the crowded lands of Connecticut and Massachusetts. Our soldier had come and chopped out a clearing and built his log house, full of hope as anyone who builds a house, I guess, and this is what it had all come to in hardly more than a hundred years.

I was standing still for a minute, thinking and quieting myself, listening to the birds and a couple of quarreling squirrels, when I heard a sound that made my heart collide with my Adam's apple.

At first it seemed like the angry snort of a large animal—a bear, or a moose, or a mountain lion (which was strictly my imagination, as none has been seen in these parts for years). When my heart settled down a bit lower than my wishbone, I realized that what I was hearing was a snore.

The growl of a mountain lion would have been less surprising. Was it man or beast? It couldn't be woman or child. Neither would be capable of that prodigious sound. I stopped being afraid. There's something near comical about a snore. How can you be shaking in your boots in the face of something that's producing a sound like that while locked, as my grandma used to say, in the arms of Morpheus?

So I started in, not stomping or anything, just sort of tippy-toe. I was really annoyed that something or someone would dare set up its bed in what was by all squatters' rights *my* cabin. Oh, all right, Willie's and my cabin, but he wasn't there to help me protest and run the varmint out.

The door, which was once in the center of the cabin, is now at the end of the side that has fallen in on itself. Fireplace and big chimney are to your left as you come in. I could see at once that the source of the noise was a huddled figure on the hearth—a figure under what had once been a bed quilt, so it was not any animal that runs wild in our mountains.

"Hey, you!" I yelled, stepping toward it, gripping my fishing pole like a baseball bat, just in case I'd need to swat whoever was lying there. I didn't get more than two feet or so into the room when *splat!* I was flat on my nose on the dirt floor, dry leaves stuck in my still-open mouth.

Pushing myself up to my knees, I looked about, a little dazed, to see what might have tripped me. It wasn't the snorer. He hadn't moved. He was just sawing away as carefree as before. Blinking the stars out of my head and accustoming my eyes to the dark, I saw behind me to my right a small, skinny form. The light from the door caught the shape of a raggedy skirt, so I knew it to be female before I heard the giggle.

"Guess I gotcha," she said when she saw I was looking straight at her.

"What are you doing trespassing in my cabin?" I asked the question with as much dignity as I could muster while spitting out leaves, brushing off my clothes, and getting to my feet.

"*Your* cabin? It ain't been nobody's cabin for a coon's age until me and Paw took possession." Scrawny as her body was, her mouth was as sassy as an overfed cat.

"Me and Willie claimed it years ago," I countered. Two makes "years." I wasn't lying. Besides, the trespassers couldn't have been here more than a few days at most.

"If it's yourn, why ain't you living in it?" she asked. "You left, and me and Paw come in and took over." She eyed me belligerently. "And don't think for one minute we're planning on leaving"—she paused and looked over at the snorer—"until we is good and ready."

"I ain't never seen you around these parts," I said. It seemed fit to match my language to hers.

"Yeah?" she said, meaning *So what?*

"That one your pa?" I asked, pointing to the snorer.

"Jest what business is that of yourn?"

"I told you," I said. "It's my cabin—me and Willie's. We come on it first."

"Prove it."

"Wal, it's got our stuff in it," I said.

"Yeah?"

66

I realized then that any apples or butternuts the animals had left would have been consumed by this pair of tramps. Likewise the corn silks. Extra fishing poles were, likely as not, part of that gray ash in the old fireplace by now. Our old shirts, dime novels, and pipes were nowhere in sight. There was no evidence I could point out, even if she'd allowed some of it to link Willie or me to this claim.

I sighed. "Wal, it *is* ours."

The snoring in front of the hearth turned into a series of snorts, a raspy cough, the loud clearing of catarrh from a clogged throat. The bundle sat up and shuddered. "Vile!" it bellowed. "Whar's my medsin?"

Neither the girl nor I moved. The bundle turned itself around with some difficulty and stared, taking in me and the girl at the same moment. "Whozat?"

"Git up, Paw," she said quietly. "Viztor come calling."

Visitor? I was the landlord. I was a little wary of the snorer once he was upright, but if I didn't put my foot down immediately, there was no telling how long they'd stay. "It's mine," I said. My voice squeaked, so I boomed out the next sentence like a bass drum. "By rights, I'm owner of this cabin."

The man began shuddering to his feet.

"It's all right, Paw. It's no more his 'an ours." She gave me a glance. "He's nothing but a little kid talking big."

The man looked me over head to toe as if measuring how big a threat I might be. I squinched my eyes to keep from blinking. He was head, shoulders, and half a chest taller than me.

To my enormous relief and small satisfaction, he broke the gaze. "We was here first," he said to the girl in what was not quite a whine.

"Yeah, Paw," she said. She put one hand on her narrow hip. "We *was* here and we *is* here. You can jest rest easy on that."

He lurched toward us. I stepped out of the way. I couldn't help it. Then I realized it was the doorway he was heading for, not me. I did another quick sidestep.

"Jest got up," he muttered. "Got to—"

She sort of shoved him out the doorway before he could finish his sentence. So there was some delicacy about her—something girllike. She watched, silent, her back to me, as he stumbled toward the trees to take care of his morning business. I was sure she didn't want me staring, so I walked in toward the hearth, pretending I was looking for something. I was embarrassed for her now, more than sorry for her. The smell of his quilt was a mixture of alcohol and vomit and filth. A drunken old fool for a father. When she turned around again to see what I was up to inside the cabin, I tried to muster up a bit of bravado. "Wal, Vile," I said.

"Violet to you," she barked. But I could tell no one in her memory had ever used her proper name. She was just trying to make herself seem a little less wretched.

I wasn't in a mood to be any kinder than I had been already. "Wal, Vile, Violet, whatever you call yourself, you're just lucky I aim to go fishing this morning. That'll give you time to eat"—she snorted—"and clear out of here before I get back." She snorted again.

We did a little dance as I tried to pass her in the doorway; then she stepped grandly aside and gave me a sweeping bow. I made a wide arc around the noise of the old man in the woods. I didn't want to stumble into him.

Seeing a spruce, I pulled out my pocketknife and pried off a patch of resin. I stuck it in my mouth. Pa says I'm going to sacrifice every tooth in my mouth to chewing resin, but it's free, and I can't afford store-bought gum. Sometimes, when you got a lot of thinking to do, you have this need to be chewing on something.

Pa. I'd hardly thought of Pa while meeting with the squatters at the cabin, but I dug my worms and reached the creek hours before Willie got there, which left me time to think. I started with the pair in the cabin, but too soon I was back home in my mind. A fellow shouldn't have too much time to ponder on things. It ain't healthy. I took a worm from my pocket and threaded most of it onto my hook. There he was, poor thing, dangling helpless from where I'd attached him. What had he ever done to me that I should treat him so cruel?

I chomped down on my wad of resin. Why did the worm make me think of Elliot? I didn't want to think of

Elliot at all, much less as a worm. There's a hymn about Jesus' dying "for such a worm as I." I didn't like that line. Elliot might be born simple, he might cause me lots of grief, but he wasn't fish bait. I chomped down harder on my resin. Usually the strong, bitter taste of it made me feel like I imagined a man chewing tobacco might feel. Now it just made me feel glummer. I wanted something sweet in my mouth like maple sugar or candy or store-bought gum.

Pa. My pa crying. Even if in general people think preachers aren't real he-men, I knew most people in Leonardstown looked up to my pa. Else why did they bluster on about their true beliefs and hint darkly that his might be inferior? Wasn't it because they knew in their hearts that he was their superior in every way that really mattered? Even Reverend Pelham had almost admitted as much. Pa's critics were like boys on the school grounds bragging about what their granddaddies did in the Great War. That don't have nothing to do with how fine a person you turned out to be yourself.

That's all bragging about your beliefs amounts to. It's just a matter of trying to assure people you got something superior that they can't see and you don't have to prove. God or no God, it don't hang on what some puny little human beings say or do or think. Any little rooster can puff out his throat and crow the morning in, and he can fool everybody including himself, long as the morning keeps on faithfully coming in on its own. The same way,

I reasoned, God, if there was a God, was going to run things His own way. He wasn't going to let mere people tell Him how to run things. God liked for people to be kind and helpful and good. No matter what the Reverend Pelham claimed, God wasn't just interested in how folks crowed.

I sat down there by the creek, and I knew all these things. I had lived for ten years in the knowledge of my pa's true strength. I didn't need to have a hero grandpa, even if I really did. As mad as I might get at him from time to time, Pa was my living hero—until I saw him put his head down on top of my mother's head and blubber like a baby.

Willie finally showed, but I was so talked out in my head, I could hardly speak out loud.

"Elliot all right?" he asked at once. "You didn't really say before."

"Elliot?" I hadn't been thinking much about Elliot just then. "Oh. Yeah. Elliot's fine. Elliot's always fine, ain't he?"

Willie looked at me funny. "Last thing I knew, he was lost."

"Pa found him." I guess I must have snapped the words out.

He was quiet for a minute, looking me over. "That's good," he said. I thought he was about to add *Ain't it?* But Willie has got sense enough not to push things. I like that quality in Willie; also that he is loyal. A friend who is loyal *and* knows when to shut up is as rare as a hippo in Cutter's Pond.

We didn't catch anything. The spring drought had been hard on fish and fishermen alike. We stayed, though, until the sun and our bellies told us that it was time for dinner.

Funny, looking back, I never mentioned to Willie anything about the cabin or its new "owners." You'd think I would have, that Willie deserved to know. Was I planning mischief even then? Something I'd be ashamed for Willie to know about? I don't think so. I just didn't quite get around to mentioning it. That's all. That's no crime, is it?

6
The Intruders

In Leonardstown most folks have their big meal in the middle of the day. The stoneworkers carry their dinner in pails to the quarry or to the shed, but originally this was a farm community, and farmers come in from the fields after a long morning of work. They need plenty to fuel themselves up for the rest of the day. Nobody in our house does farm work, but we follow the customs of the town. It makes us more a part of the community, though to tell the truth, we've never been quite a part of it. Neither of my parents was born here, for one thing. There are no grandparents or aunts and uncles in easy hailing distance when things go wrong or you want to celebrate. Pa's parents are both dead, and Ma's live up in the northeast corner of the state, away from the rail line. It's a long day's journey from here.

The family had already gathered around the table when I got home. I scurried for my place, which is next to Beth's, at the kitchen table. As I sat down, she pinched her nose, her little finger curling in the air like a comma. "Phew," she said.

"Elizabeth!" Ma was shocked to hear Beth using such an unladylike word.

"I can't help it, Mama. Please make him change. He smells like a dead fish."

"How could I? I didn't catch nothin'."

"Anything," said Pa.

I think Ma was more annoyed at Beth than she was at me, but she made me go change anyhow. Honest, sometimes the burden of having a sister who's a lady-in-training is more than a boy should have to bear.

Ma had fixed up beans and boiled some ham, almost like it was still a holiday. We all tried to eat to please her, but it was a hot day and no one was really hungry. Except Elliot. Ma watched him shovel in those beans, her eyes shining like she was proud of some big accomplishment the boy had managed.

Pa made appreciative noises over the food, but I could tell he was no hungrier than me. There were dark shadows under his eyes, making them look old and puffy. Whether from lack of sleep or crying I didn't want to guess. I kept harping on those tears. I didn't mean to, but it really shook me to see my pa so small and scared, a little boy who's hurt and running to his ma.

Beth kept turning and giving me queer looks.

"What?" I said finally. She was making me feel prickly and guilty.

Everyone turned to me like I needed to explain myself. "Tell Beth to stop looking at me," I said. I couldn't believe the stupid words that just jumped out of my mouth. I turned as red as a flag stripe.

"I can't help looking," she said sarcastically. "You're just too pretty for words."

I jumped up from the table. Pretty? I've given bloody noses for less than that.

"Sit down, Robbie," Pa said quietly. "And calm down, both of you." I gave Beth a smirk, in case she missed the point that I wasn't the only one out of line.

Willie couldn't fish after dinner. His aunt had him working the vegetable patch. Sometimes I help Willie with his chores, but that day I just couldn't make myself. Elliot was going to help Pa in our garden, so I wasn't needed at home. Or wanted. At least that was the way I was seeing it.

Without thinking, I headed back up to the cabin. Nobody was there. I called out, gently at first. When no one answered, I went on inside. There was enough light now to see around. The squatters had a couple of quilts, ragged and filthy to be sure, but still quilts. They must have built a fire sometime earlier, as there were ashes still smoldering in the old stone fireplace.

I tried to figure where they got their food. They could have marched down the hill into town and bought it same as most of us, but somehow I sensed that wasn't how they did things. I'd never seen anyone, not even the Pepin children, whose pa died in a quarry accident, look as needy as Vile did. At school, sitting close together near the wood stove, the Pepin children smelled different from us. Here in the cabin, that odor, which I could only guess was the smell of poor folks, was multiplied ten times. It made me want to gag.

There was a big kerchief by one of the quilts, tied up, I guessed to protect their worldly goods. My fingers itched to unknot those corners. What would people like Vile and her pa carry from place to place? Where had they come from? What did they call themselves? Not Gypsies, I was sure.

There was a Gypsy caravan that camped in the flats south of town every September. They'd stay a week or so. We boys loved to go and spy on them. Their wagons were painted in bright colors. Their clothes were motley colored, too. Both the men and women wore gold in their ears. They made me think of Solomon in all his glory. When Ned Watson said they kidnapped babies and ate them, I knocked him down. "Wal, you're one baby they'd spit out," I said.

At night, around their fires, the Gypsy folk sang songs, the likes of which you'd never hear in any church—wild songs that would make your blood race and sad tunes that would make you feel lonely and homesick even when you couldn't understand a word. I liked the horses best. They were smaller than Morgans or any farm horse I had ever seen. But they weren't ponies. They were too proud to be ponies—and decorated as beautifully as the people. Nobody who had such wonderful little horses could be evil. I was sure of that.

No, Vile and her pa were no kin to Gypsies. More's the pity.

Were they then what some folks had taken to calling "hoboes"? Pa wouldn't let us use that word. He said it insulted honest men who had been thrown out of work when times got bad, as they had too often in the last few years. How blessed—Pa never used the word *lucky*—how blessed we were that the quarries had stayed in production, making it possible for the farmers to sell their produce and for most of us in this part of Vermont to eat regular. But even if I was allowed to use the word *hobo*, Vile couldn't be one. I'd never heard of little girl hoboes—just grown men.

"Thief! I caught you!"

Vile was standing over me. I looked up startled. The huge form of her pa—he was full and tall as mine—filled the door. His right arm was behind his back, as though he was hiding something.

"Thief!" Vile said again. I looked down and saw that while my mind had been picturing Gypsies and hoboes, my hands had been untying the ends of the kerchief. Vile fell to her knees and snatched it out from under my hand, but not before I spied printed papers—like bills that get posted up to advertise performances and revival meetings or criminals on the loose. I had no time to read anything. Vile had snatched the whole bundle and was busily retying it, mumbling under her breath at me.

"I didn't take nothing," I whispered. I wasn't anxious for her pa to hear me. "Honest." What things of theirs did she imagine I could possibly want?

"You was fixing to," she said. "You would have if me and Paw hadn't caught you in the very act."

"I was just curious," I mumbled, then wished I hadn't. It made me seem worse than a thief, poking about in their meager possessions, as though because they had so few things, they had no right to keep private what they did have.

She finished knotting the kerchief, pulling the ends tight with her rough little hands. The nails were bitten, rimmed in black. By this time the man had come into the cabin, dragging behind him a burlap bag. He reached for the bundle with his free hand. It, too, was raw and red with filthy nails. I couldn't help but think of my father's strong, clean hands.

"What you doin' back here agin?" he asked. He was close enough now for me to see the dark red of his nose and the broken blue veins cobwebbing his face.

"This was—is—my cabin."

"We'll believe that when we see your bill of sale." Vile hawked and spit on the dirt floor like a hanger-on in the livery stable. I'd never seen a girl with such a dirty face. Her whole visible body was a strange shade of gray. She saw my look, snuffled, then wiped her nose on the back of her hand. "You can stop staring. Or didn't your momma tell you no manners?"

I could feel the red start at the roots of my hair. "My ma—"

"Git!" the man said, as though I was a stray dog.

"I didn't mean no harm. Really." I wiped my sweaty palms down the sides of my britches. "Look, if you need a better place to stay or—or anything—my pa's the preacher at the Congregational church—he'd be glad to—"

"We do jest fine, Mr. Prissy Preacher Pants," Vile said. "Jest fine. You heard what Paw said. Git."

"But what will you eat? There ain't nothing here."

The man's eyes shifted sidewise. So that was it. They were stealing food. I couldn't be too self-righteous on that score. Me and Willie often took apples and butter-nuts—all the fellows did. But more for sport, not to keep from starving. Besides, it was only the fifth of July. There's not much ripe this early in Vermont.

At that moment the burlap bag that the man was dragging behind him gave out a loud *bwraaaak*.

I forgot to be scared. "I'll be snackered," I said. "You got a chicken in there."

As though to answer me, the bag began to hop about and holler.

They closed ranks in front of the suddenly lively sack. It jumped and squawked to a fare-thee-well.

I couldn't help it. I started to laugh.

"Hush up!" I couldn't tell if the girl's command was for me or the chicken.

"How'd you get past Webster's dogs?" I asked.

Her eyes narrowed. I had the upper hand now. "You ain't thinking to tell on us?"

"Naw. I ain't no snitch." Then, to assure them—and myself?—whose side I was on: "Want some carrots and a potato or two to cook with it?"

The girl was still giving me the suspicious eye, but the man pitched the kerchief-wrapped bundle into the corner and gave me a nod. "Vile, go fetch us some water. The boy may be some use to us after all." He turned and gave me what I could only figure out was his idea of a friendly smile. "Name's Zeb," he said, holding out his big dirty paw.

I gave him my hand. Somehow I couldn't make myself give him my name as well, so I rechristened myself on the spot. "Fred," I said, quickly disentangling from his handshake. But I liked my new name. I always thought I should have been named Fred.

"Fred here will fetch the roots"—he gave me his smarmy smile—"while I remove the squawk from this here bird." With that he reached into the sack, grabbed the chicken by its neck, and twirled it around and around over his head like a lasso in a Wild West Show.

My mouth fell open wide as a bear cave, in awe or horror, I couldn't say which. "I reckon you don't need me to bring the ax, then," I said faintly.

"Not hardly," he said. His laugh showed me a mouthful of missing and rotting teeth.

I took to my heels and skedaddled down the hill. The winter vegetables, what was left of them, were down in the root cellar. It seemed strange to be stealing something that Ma would have gladly given me had I asked. But asking would mean explanations, and explanations would mean giving away the whereabouts of me and Willie's hideaway and the fact that two of the world's most needy thieves were tucked away up there.

I'm not sure why I didn't want to tell on them. Mainly because I pride myself that I am not a snitch. But I could tell about them without including the thief part. All the tramps who came to our door in hard times got hot meals and, if they were willing, work to do. None to my knowledge had ever hung around more than a week. They all figured there'd be better pickings down the road, I reckon.

Anyhow, just like a Union spy, I watched the manse until I saw Ma step off the kitchen porch with her market basket over her arm. Beth followed after, dragging Letty, who was intent on observing something in the grass near the steps and not eager to get on down the path.

I waited until the whole little procession turned down off School Street onto West Hill Road before I sneaked down the hill. Pa and Elliot seemed safely engaged at the far end of the garden, but I kept a sharp ear out anyway as I crept into the house and down the cellar stairs.

Our cellar is all bounded about with huge granite boulders, which form the foundation of the manse. It's almost pitch-dark down there—just a tiny slit of a window at the bottom of the stairs. It smells dank like I guess the inside of a tomb might. Sometimes when I go down there, I pretend I'm the first archaeologist to go inside a pyramid. Willie hates that. It really spooks him.

I felt my way into the root cellar. I could tell the carrots by shape. This time of year they're dried and sort of bumpy. They taste reedy, too, but cooked up, they aren't too bad even if Letty tries to spit them out. The potatoes are soft and sprouting by May, not to mention July, but it couldn't be helped. That was all I had to offer. I stuffed the pockets of my britches until they bulged and flowed over. Then I headed around the granite wall toward the stairs.

"Robbie? Whatcha doin'?"

I jumped like a flushed rabbit. Elliot was standing on the top step, peering down into the dark. I hadn't heard him at all. Big and clumsy as he is, sometimes he can be quiet as a cat.

"Nothin'," I snapped, starting up the stairs. "Nothin' that's any business of yours." I pushed past him and headed through the kitchen for the porch door.

"Where you goin'?"

"Uh—fishing."

"Can I go, too, huh, Robbie?"

I tried hard to tamp down my impatience as I cupped

my hands over my bulging pockets. "Maybe later," I said. "Say? Don't I hear Pa calling you?"

He cocked his ear to the silence. "Pa found me," he said.

"Yeah, Elliot. I know."

"Why you mad at me, Robbie?"

I could feel the gorge rise in my throat. "Why should I be mad at you?"

"I dunno. Shumtime you are, Robbie. I don' know why. Was I bad?"

I sighed. "No, Elliot. You was just lost. We was worried about you."

"Not bad?" he asked anxiously.

"No. Just not careful where you was going."

"Pa found me," he said, then worried all over again. "He cried."

"I know."

"Was he shad he foun' me?"

"No, Elliot, he was happy."

"Den why he cry?"

"Maybe he was really tired out."

"Oh." He seemed to ponder the idea. I opened the porch door and started out.

"Don' get los'," he called after me.

"I won't."

"Promish?"

"Promise."

7
Thou Shalt Not Steal

The hill behind our house, which is really part of Webster's pastureland, is terraced by generations of cows meandering across it. Cows, as you might guess, don't fancy sliding headfirst down a slope like a child on a sled. They like to take the long road home, thus the zigzag cow paths. As often as I climb that hill, I still have to pay attention. But that afternoon I had the feeling someone was following me, and I tripped more than once, climbing as I was with one eye over my shoulder to see what might be at my back.

I kept wishing I'd taken time to put the vegetables in a sack or basket. It's hard to move with any speed whilst carrots and potatoes bump and poke at your thighs. Once I commenced to run, and a potato just popped out of my pocket and started rolling down the hill. It bounced on a dried cow pie and just kept going. I had to chase after it, and when I did, most of the rest of the potatoes hopped out and joined the fun. I was breathing hard by the time I corralled the whole shebang or as many as I could run down. I slowed to an uphill crawl, holding my hands tight against my pockets to keep the blooming roots in place while I engineered across the cow-paths and around the sharpest rocks and sidestepped the wettest of the cow pies that decorate the pasture.

Let me tell you, I was in some kind of sweat before I hit the sugar bush that rimmed the woods. The cool under the trees was more than welcome.

I smelled the smoke before I could see it rising from the stone chimney of the cabin. The hoboes? Tramps?— I'll just call them Vile and Zeb—had built a big fire. They had a pot of water going. I guess they always carried a pot with them. Willie and I didn't have one. But maybe they'd got it the same way they'd got the chicken. I wasn't about to ask.

"Dadblasted water," Zeb was growling. "It hain't never gonna bile. Hell would freeze over quicker. Pour some out, Vile. I'm hungry as a bear."

"You got to have enough boiling to dunk the whole bird, Pa. Else the feathers won't yank easy." She spied me about then. "Well, if it ain't Ned. Didn't speck to see you again."

"Fred," I corrected her, "Fred. I told you I was coming back. Look here. I brung the taters and carrots like I promised."

"Now, that's a good boy, hain't it, Vile?" Zeb said, but I could tell from the look on Vile's face she didn't think I was so good.

I laid out the vegetables on a blackened window frame. There was no furniture in the cabin. Vile came over and inspected my wrinkled brown carrots and soft, sprouting potatoes. She snorted in disdain.

"That's the best we got," I said bristling. "New carrots ain't ready, and Pa only digs new potatoes as we need them."

"I reckon you figure they'd be too tasty for the likes of us," she said.

"Shet your mouth, Vile," the man said. "The boy done what he could."

She sniffed, but turned her attention to the fire. Finally the water began to hum and then to bubble. Zeb picked up the dead hen by her yellow feet and poked her—glazed eyes, head, and broken neck first—into the boiling water until her whole feathered body had been dunked. Then he handed the wet hen to Vile. She took it outdoors and began to pluck out the feathers.

I waited for Zeb to throw out the dirty water they'd doused the chicken in and start fresh, but no, Zeb just took it off the pot hook and set it on the hearth so it wouldn't all boil away. "You gonna peel them taters, Ed?" he asked. "Or jest gaze at the scenery?"

I stuck my hand in my pocket. Then I remembered Ma making me change my britches before dinner. "I ain't got my pocketknife," I said. He took something off the mantel and pitched it at me. I jumped out of the way, making him laugh. It was a great horn-handled jackknife.

I hid my red face, leaning to pick it up. The blade, when I pulled it out, was rusty and crusted with filth. I ran it back and forth across the side of my britches making him laugh again. It was awkward trying to peel with it. I was taking out hunks of potato flesh along with the skin.

"There ain't gonna be no tater left, rate you're going," Zeb said.

Vile poked her head in the door and watched me a minute. "Here," she said, handing her father the bird, "you finish this. I'll peel." She took the knife from my hand. "You cut jest like a boy," she said, finishing the job skillfully as Ma. "Now, hand me them carrots."

I fetched her the old bumpy carrots.

"Look worse'n your taters," she said.

"I'll wash them," I said, and raced out to the spring before she could stop me.

There was just a trickle and a little mud puddle to indicate where most Julys a lively spring burst the soil and ran down to meet the creek which joined the North Branch south of town. How would Vile and Zeb live if it dried up completely? I washed the carrots as best I could. They didn't look much better—still brown and lumpy. But I couldn't be blamed for that, could I? I dawdled at the spring, washed my own face and hands, knelt and put my mouth down near the trickle and got a mouthful of water. Vile must have the patience of Job to wait for a whole pot's worth.

When I got back to the cabin, they had already given

me up. "Thought you'd taken those pitiful roots hostage and headed west," Zeb said.

"Naw. Run home to his mama, more's the likely," Vile said.

I ignored her and handed Zeb the carrots. He threw them, green stub, peel and all into the pot which was already scumming over from chicken juice. I couldn't tell if they'd even gutted the bird. They sure hadn't removed the head or the feet. I looked away. I didn't want to see those glassy eyes staring at me from the pot. Seemed like a cannibal stew.

"Wal," I said as casually as I could manage, "we got prayer meeting tonight. Best be on my way. Sorry I can't stay for supper."

"Who asked you?" Vile snapped.

It was my plan to stay away from the cabin. There was plenty for me and Willie to do elsewhere. But Willie's aunt would not cooperate. Anytime I came by during the next week, she found some chore for Willie to do. I guess she was anxious to keep Willie's soul out of mortal danger, since the Devil has so much work for idle hands. I was the preacher's boy, so she didn't say it outright, but she gave me the distinct impression that, lazy as I always seemed to be, she considered me a prime candidate for the Devil's payroll.

I was rereading *Kidnapped* for the fourth time, which was fine entertainment early in the day but by dinnertime Elliot's and my room, which is on the third floor and has two big windows to the southwest, gets hot as Hades. If I went downstairs, Ma could not seem to help herself finding me something to do. I give her credit. She never hangs "the Devil has work for idle hands" over my head, but the end result is mighty similar. She'll need me to look after Letty for just a minute while she runs an errand, or ask if I would take Elliot fishing, or, if Pa happens to emerge from the study, suggests that he'd appreciate another hand in the garden.

Truth be told, I don't think Pa really fancies me as a fellow gardener. I think he prefers Elliot, who is content to do exactly as he's told and doesn't ask questions. Sometimes I watch Pa yank out weeds and wonder if he's named each one after a troublesome parishioner. He gets so much satisfaction tearing those roots from the soil and knocking all the dirt from the roots. For a man who can hardly bear to spank a child, he sure does enjoy beating on those weeds.

Ma says I have an overactive imagination, but I don't think I'm just fancying this, because one Monday morning I was watching him pull at a really stubborn weed, falling near over when it came loose. As he was smacking it hard against the ground to loosen the dirt, I said, innocent as a newborn lamb, "Deacon Slaughter was sure riled up about your praying for the Filipinos yesterday, wasn't he?" His face turned red as a winter sunset. I know a guilty face when I see it. Still, guilt doesn't seem at home on Pa's face. It creeps up and sneaks around uncomfortably, as though even guilt knows this is a man who is pure of heart—just one who's been pushed past human limits.

Politics have been giving Pa trouble for some time. First there was the war in Cuba to end Spanish tyranny, which Pa, smart as he is, didn't have the gumption not to question out loud. I had a hard time blaming Deacon Slaughter on that one. When Vermont boys is signing up to die, even preachers got to talk patriotic, don't they?

But Pa really got riled up when President McKinley decided as long as we were stomping out Spanish tyranny in Cuba, we might just as well drive the Spaniards out of Asia while we were at it. So he sends Admiral Dewey, who is lazing around the Pacific with nothing much to do, over to the Philippines. And a few months later those Filipinos, that our battleships have gone to save, they get uppity and start trying to save themselves from us. And Admiral Dewey, a good Vermonter, by the way, who is out there doing his best for Old Glory, not to mention the end of Spanish tyranny, suddenly finds himself fighting the very people he's come to rescue. And my pa can't seem to help praying for the Filipinos.

Even though I couldn't bring myself to ask him directly why he kept praying for the misery of the Filipino people to end, I guess he thought he owed me an explanation.

"They just want their freedom, Robbie. They may

not think American guns are all that different from Spanish guns."

But they're a *lot* different, aren't they? I mean, we're America—Land of the Free and Home of the Brave. Then I thought about slavery and the Great War. But it was only the South that was wrong. Lots of Vermont boys fought and died to free the slaves. Good thing Pa was too young to be a preacher in *that* war. He'd probably prayed for the miseries of Johnny Reb.

Finally I couldn't stand it anymore. "But I don't understand, Pa. Why do you got to pray for our enemies?"

He was full red in the face now, but he looked me straight in the eye. "Because the Lord commanded me to," he said.

I couldn't say anything after that. Could you? Pa's not one of these preachers always bragging he got a direct telegraph cable hooked up to Heaven. If he tells you, "The Lord commanded me to," you can't argue it, even if you want to. You know the man ain't given to idle boasts.

Anyhow, that all happened a while back. My immediate concern was the present. It was a perfect July afternoon. If the Devil has work for idle hands, he was waving his flag, beating his drum, blowing his trumpet to recruit the likes of me, a boy with nothing to do on a lazy summer afternoon.

I thought about heading up to Webster's orchard and

pinching some green apples. But it's no fun stealing apples on your own. You got to have someone on watch and someone to creep to the trees, someone to giggle with and exclaim how close you come to being caught, someone to agree on how good they taste—those hard sour little stones that make your eyes water and your mouth pucker to a kiss. If Ma served them for supper, we'd swear she was out to poison us.

There was no use complaining to Ma that there was nothing to do. You can be sure she'd remedy that. And I had no wish to take Elliot fishing. He'd had enough attention to last him a couple of weeks. Or she might take a notion to suggest I read something besides a novel—something to improve my mind. Now, you know I like to read, but somehow the minute somebody suggests that reading might improve my mind, the best book in the world takes on the taste of castor oil. I don't want to improve my mind any time of year. In July it seems downright criminal.

I wandered out onto the porch, where most of the old newspapers are stacked, and looked at the ads for bicycles to daydream a bit. Not that it would do any good. I showed Pa the ad in last week's paper that said Nichols was giving them away, and he just laughed. "Nichols thinks twenty dollars is giving wheels away," he said. Pa makes less than ninety dollars a month. When times are hard (which times always seem to be), Pa gets most of his pay in produce. You can't help that if you're a preacher, but I didn't fancy Nichols taking a bushel of last year's root-cellar vegetables in exchange for a bicycle, new or used. Still, dreams are free, right?

When I start on a printed page, I tend to eat it down like a peppermint stick. It didn't matter that the *Tyler Times* I was reading was three weeks old. Nothing had changed in baseball. Boston was still battling Brooklyn for first place in the league. I swear. God makes you a Beaneater fan just to teach you patient endurance. Or make you suffer. One or the other. There is no joy involved whatsoever. Marion Clark "who disappeared in the arms of her nurse" was still missing, as was the nurse. In this issue of the *Times,* however, a new reward had been announced. Apparently the New York newspaper and other folks down there had put together a reward of $3,500 for the baby's safe return. Three thousand five hundred dollars!

Suddenly I was wide awake. I began tearing through the next stack. I needed to know if that reward was still being offered. I mean, it wasn't impossible to imagine that that so-called nurse might be lurking around Leonardstown right this minute. It was the perfect hiding place. No one from New York City *ever* came here. I couldn't find the most recent papers on the porch, but there was another stack of papers in the wood box by the kitchen stove.

I shuffled through them, my hands shaking. Tarnation. They'd found Marion Clark barely a week before and returned her to her grieving loved ones. Someone had already claimed that fortune. But, hey, here was another kidnapping. New York was some dangerous city. A boy this time. Seems he just wandered off from his parents. Next thing they knew, here came a ransom note demanding $1,000 for his return. So one way or another there was a fortune to be made in the kidnapping business.

Now if only someone would get themselves kidnapped in Leonardstown, I was sure to be the one to find them. Shoot! For $3,500 I could forget about a bicycle. I'd go for a whole fleet of motorcars! I didn't consider kidnapping someone to demand ransom. Who'd want to take care of somebody else's brat while waiting around for them to get the cash together? Besides, I hadn't been an apeist long enough to commit crime on a scale that exceeded the Ten Commandments to that extent. If they caught you for kidnapping, you'd probably swing. Even if they didn't decide to hang you, they'd surely throw you in jail for the rest of your natural life. I didn't fancy either end. I turned the page and went back to staring at the ads for wheels.

That night I couldn't get to sleep. As hot and stuffy as my third-floor room was, it was probably cold up at the cabin and dark as pitch. We wouldn't have a moon, even a sliver of one, till tomorrow night. Those raggedy quilts were all they had for cover. I ought to have told

94

them to get some pine boughs or leaves to lay between themselves and the earth floor.

Where had they come from? Had they ever been respectable townsfolk who sat in a pew at the Congregational church or stood up to speak in a town meeting? It was hard to imagine. Still, they hadn't always hid out in abandoned cabins—just the two of them. Vile looked to be about my age, ten, or at the most eleven. She was born somewhere. Once she'd had a mother. I tried to picture a dirty, ragged woman and set her amongst them. It made me shiver despite the leftover heat the day had stored up in my room. I reached down and pulled up my summer quilt and snuggled under it.

Vile was for Violet. How did she go from flower to dirt? I'd never seen anyone so poor. The poorest child in Leonardstown had a roof over his head and a school to go to. Even the children whose fathers had died young from working in granite and whose mothers had too many children and no wages coming in could count on the town. The town still made sure you had a roof and food. It might be on the town poor farm where nobody really wanted to go, but still that was better than what Vile and Zeb had, wasn't it?

I might be a conscienceless apeist who didn't have to obey the commandments, but that didn't mean I had lost all human feeling. I decided to persuade Vile and Zeb to come to town. Pa would help them. What kind of work would Zeb be able to do? He didn't look smart enough to work in the quarry or in the stone sheds. It might have to be the poor farm, at least for a while. How could they be too proud to go to the poor farm? They were squatting in an abandoned cabin, stealing what food they had. Wasn't the town farm better than jail? Which was sure where Zeb was headed if he snatched one chicken too many. He wasn't oversmart. The law was sure to catch up with him soon.

I didn't sleep all that well. When I did fall asleep, it was to dream. In the dream I didn't have Ma and Pa anymore. I was living with Zeb and Vile. They made me do the stealing for them because I was smarter than Zeb, and Vile was a girl.

The night was hot and seemed to press in on me as I crept down to Mr. Webster's chicken house. It was so still, I could hear my own loud breathing. But then, just as I grabbed a bird, all the hens began to squawk, the dogs commenced to bark, and Webster came yelling out of the house with his shotgun.

"Don't shoot!" I was crying like a baby. "It's only me, Robbie Hewitt!"

Mr. Webster cocked his eye at me. It was clear he didn't recognize me. He raised the gun and sighted.

"Mr. Webster!" I cried out. "It's me, Robbie Hewitt, the preacher's boy!"

I heard the crash of the shot. Everything went black. Then I could feel a warm, thick liquid oozing up and spreading across my chest. I knew I was dead.

I sat up in bed. I couldn't breathe. I just sat there gasping for air. What I wanted to do was run down the stairs to Ma and Pa's bedroom and crawl into their big bed with them, but I couldn't do that. I was nearly eleven years old.

It was only a dream, I told myself. Just a bad dream. I forced myself to lie down again. Was it a warning dream like in the Bible? People got warned in dreams. Maybe it meant I shouldn't go near the cabin again, shouldn't let myself get messed up with the likes of Zeb and Vile. That was it. I'd just stay away, and they couldn't hurt me. I lay down and put my hand over my heart until I could feel that it was slowing back down to normal. Then I turned over and finally went to sleep.

Thou Shalt Not Kill

Next day I helped Willie with his chores. I could tell he was puzzled by my sudden attack of industry, but he wasn't going to ask nosy questions and scare me off. He chopped the wood himself. He said it took me too long, and I never split it even. He sent me to pull weeds from the carrot bed. We needed rain bad. I broke off most of the weeds at ground level, the ground was so hard and dry.

"I think we should water these vegetables some," I yelled to Willie.

"Can't!" he yelled back. "The well's low." He was right. It would be worse to have no drinking and cooking water than to lose a few carrots. He took another swing, cracking a log neatly down the middle. He set up one of the halves and split it.

"Say," I said, coming over to where he worked. "Why don't we hike over to the pond and take a dip after you're done?"

His eyes lit up. "Shhh," he warned. "Don't let Aunt Millie hear you."

We took our fishing poles to pretend we might be bringing home dinner, but once we were out of sight, we laid them down beside the road and took off flying down the hill to Main Street, south to Cutter's Pond Road, and out into the countryside below the eastern hills.

The smell of summer, even a dry and dusty one, is perfume to a boy's nostrils. The pastures with grass and even cow dung . . . the fields of hay . . . the dust puffing up from the road under our bare feet . . .

"Wait." Willie was panting and holding his side. "I got a stitch."

"Sissy!" I hollered, running on. True, I hadn't split a pile of wood that morning. But I would have kept running even so. The faster I ran, the farther behind I left the demons that had been at my heels for days. No more Zeb. No more Vile. No more Reverend Pelham or Deacon Slaughter. No more Elliot.

If I stopped pounding down the road long enough to think straight, I would have been ashamed, but I wasn't going to think—just slap down my bare sun-browned feet till they were lost in the dust of the road.

I didn't run the whole mile and a half. That was too much even for me that day. Still, I reached the pond long before Willie did. I threw myself on the huge flat rock at the south end that belonged to us boys by right of conquest, lay back, and let the sun bake my face. My limbs melted and I was nearly asleep by the time Willie came laboring up, still holding his side. He was breathing so hard, I could barely make out the words, but he was jabbering like a blue jay at me, full of excuses as to why he couldn't keep up. I just lay there, my face warm, my body still as the face of the pond. For that little while it felt as if all was right with the world.

Sometime later, after Willie had calmed himself down, we stripped to our birthday suits and dove off the rock. The coldness shocked our warm skin, but in a pleasing, bracing kind of way. I turned over on my back, spewing out a mouthful of water at the sky in my whale imitation. Then, forgetting even to show off, I just hovered there, feeling as though I was one of the clouds, floating lazily in the blue.

Long minutes later we climbed back up on the rock and fell asleep in the sun.

"Hey there, fellers! Havin' a nice nap?"

We both woke with a start and grabbed for our clothes, which were no longer there. Out in the middle of the pond Tom and Ned Weston were treading water, paddling with one hand, while holding something in the air with the other. "Need these?" Tom called, waving what looked like Willie's shirt and britches. Ned laughed and waved mine.

"Don't you dare!" I yelled. Willie didn't stop to yell, he just dove in and headed for Tom Weston as fast as he could swim. "Don't you dare!" I yelled once more before I dove in.

"Nyeh! Nyeh! Nyeh!" Ned waved my clothes toward me, but before I could get halfway across, he turned and hurled his bundle as far away toward the other side as he could. Then Tom threw his, but Willie had nearly caught up, and he grabbed his shirt and britches before they sank. Willie didn't wear underwear in the summer. He swam back to shore and pitched his soaking clothes up on the rock, then started out to help me find mine.

I had swum to the spot where Ned had thrown them. There was nothing to be seen, not even underwear. I dove over and over again. Each time I surfaced, I could hear Ned's "Nyeh! Nyeh! Nyeh!" They were both screaming with laughter.

"Forget them, Robbie," Willie was saying. I guess he could see something roiling in my face every time I came up for air.

Finally we gave up. It was no use keeping on. The pond was at least thirty feet deep in the center. "You little rat!" I yelled at Ned.

"Whatcha need clothes for, Robbie? Ain't you a monkey's boy?"

Tom began to laugh. "That's what his daddy thinks!"

"And he's got a brother to prove it, too!" Then Ned began to sing: "Wha a fen we ha in Sheeshush! Aw our shins and grease to bear!"

"Shut up, Ned!" I yelled. "Shut up!"

"Monkey sons! Monkey brothers! Monkey papa! Monkey boys—"

By this time the blood was raging between my ears. I swam like fury over to Ned Weston, and in the middle of his chant, I reached over and shoved him facedown in the water. He was flailing his arms. Tom and Willie both yelled at me. But I didn't let up.

Willie started toward us, crying out as he came, "Stop it, Robbie!"

I forced Ned's stupid little pointed head deeper into the water.

Willie snatched my hand and pushed me away. When Ned came sputtering up to the surface, still flailing, Willie hooked his arm around Ned's neck and held him up. Tom, looking scared and dazed, swam up to them. No one said a word. Still towing Ned, Willie turned his back on me and headed for the shore. Tom followed them in.

I watched from a distance as the two of them helped Ned onto land. The Weston boys pulled on their britches and, still buttoning their shirts, started for home. Willie put on his own sopping clothes, never raising his eyes to where I was treading water. It took me a minute to figure it out. He was fixing to leave me there stark naked.

"Hey!" I yelled, splashing for the shore. "Willie, wait!"

He glanced over his shoulder at me. I didn't like the look on his face.

I clambered out. I'd never been so aware of being naked in my life. "I wouldn'ta killed him. You know that."

"How could I know it?" he asked, so softly I could barely hear him.

"What? C'mon, Willie. You know me." My skin was all gooseflesh. "You don't think for a minute . . ."

He gave me a look—anger and pain mixed. "How can you know what a feller will do? One who don't have to pay no mind to the Ten Commandments?"

I stood there naked, shaking in the sun, my mouth wide open. "Willie! You know me," I protested. But I didn't know myself. A flood of horror washed over me. I *had* meant to kill Ned Weston. I could deny it to the day I died, but I knew I'd felt the rage boiling in my head that proved me kin to every murderer in history from Cain to Jack the Ripper.

"Still," said Willie, "they had no business mocking Elliot, much less your pa."

I jerked my head to agree, but I couldn't make myself look him in the eye.

"How're you gonna get home—like that?"

A quick glance assured me that he wasn't smiling. I should have known. Willie's too kind a soul to pile up on a person's despair. "Here," he said, unbuttoning his shirt. "You're turning blue. Put this on at least." He handed me his shirt. Willie's shirt barely scraped my privates, but it was better than nothing.

"What am I gonna do?" I asked him miserably. He thought I meant about being naked, but I meant way more than that.

"There's the icehouse," he said. "You can wait in there till I can fetch you some more clothes."

Ma and Pa. I thought my heart had sunk as low as it could, but it plunged into an even deeper gorge. What would they think of me? They'd know soon enough. Mr. Earl Weston was probably halfway to my house by now, nonetheless—"I don't want my folks—"

"Don't worry, Robbie," he said kindly. "I ain't as dumb as you think."

I wanted to deny it, but he was right. I did think I was smarter than him. I guess I thought I was the smartest boy in Leonardstown—nearly. Well, look what it got me—bare bottomed as a pig and blushing like a girl. And ashamed as Judas Iscariot.

The icehouse stands on the north side of the pond. Every winter the Cutters saw blocks of ice and store them, each layer covered in sawdust, in a pit in the center of the house. Then, come summer, they make a fortune selling ice to everyone in Leonardstown.

There were no windows in the wooden shack, only a door. It wasn't locked. Willie and me went in. Now I really began to shiver. By the light from the doorway I saw there was a splintery stool on one side under where the tongs and picks and ice saws were hanging. It made me feel a little like I was in a butcher shop, more like the meat than a customer.

"I'll need my shirt."

"What?"

"I'm sorry, Robbie, but I can't walk into town half naked."

He was right, of course, but I sure hated to give up what little protection his shirt afforded. I took it off and handed it back. "Hurry, won't you?"

"Fast as I can manage it," he promised. He shut the door after him, leaving me plunged in complete blackness. I worked my way along the wall to where the stool was. I didn't want to fall into the ice pit by mistake. I felt for the tongs and picks and then found a space of clear wall I could safely lean against. The splintery stool didn't seem inviting to bare buttocks.

Outside, a bird called and another answered. They sounded happy and full of life. I got tired of leaning. Besides, the wall was rough and could share its splinters as well as the stool could. I tried sitting on the cold dirt floor but had to get up soon. Mostly I stood on one foot and then the other. Time had no meaning in the darkness. Even after my eyes got accustomed to it and I could see tiny bits of daylight through the chinks in the wall, I felt as though I had been confined in that dark dungeon forever. I didn't dare to crack the door. Suppose some more of the boys came to swim? Suppose Mr. Weston sent the sheriff to arrest me? Suppose Pa came looking for me?

I tried not to think. Everything that came to my mind twisted my stomach. What did the Weston boys mean calling Pa and Elliot monkeys? Was their father accusing Pa of believing in evolution? I knew that word, all right.

It was the worst thing you could do even if you weren't a preacher—to believe that man wasn't created by God on the sixth day but had descended from the apes.

Even to someone who had decided not to believe in God—even to an avowed unbeliever like me—the idea of having a monkey for an ancestor was disgusting. Just because they had faces like people didn't mean we were kin, for goodness' sake. A thrush and a vulture both have wings, but that doesn't make them kissing cousins.

To taunt me, which those boys did love to do, even to taunt me that my pa would be so stupid and godless as to entertain the possibility—and then to take poor Elliot as proof—even in a joking way . . . They had no right! . . .

Dear God. I had nearly killed Ned Weston. . . . I began to breathe funny. I was freezing cold and sweating at the same time. Oh, Willie, I begged, hurry up. Please. I wanted out of that dark shed even if I had no place to go. I needed clothes. But after that—after I put my clothes on—then what? It wasn't just the fear of Mr. Weston or the sheriff. It was Pa. The shame I would bring him. Mabel Cramm's bloomers were nothing compared . . .

Dok dok dok. Who in Hades was knocking? I stooped down, squatting as close to the ground as I could, my breath so loud, I was sure it would give me away.

The door was gently pushed open a few inches. I waited, my eyes on the dark form in the crack.

"Robbie? You dere?"

Elliot? What was he doing here? I was furious. What was Willie thinking, getting Elliot mixed up in this?

"Robbie?" he called again in his soft, tentative voice, pushing the door open just wide enough to squeeze in. He started forward.

"Watch it!" I jumped up to grab him. I didn't want him stepping into the ice pit.

"Robbie! You scare' me!"

"Stay right by the door," I ordered hoarsely, returning to my dark spot. "There's a big hole in the floor."

"Aw right," he whispered, blinking like an owl. "You naked, Robbie," he said at last.

"Don't stare," I said. "It ain't polite."

"Sorry, Robbie. Oh." He held out a little bundle. "Willie shay I gotta bring closh to you?" His voice went up in a question.

I took a step forward to take the clothes. In the light from the door my skin gleamed white.

"You *really* naked," he said.

"Just gimme my clothes, Elliot, and stop staring, okay?"

"Sorry, Robbie," he said, snuffling his very drippy nose.

"Where's Willie?" I asked, dressing as fast as I could. "Why didn't he bring these himself?"

"Mr. Weshum come callin'. Willie shay he ha' go home. He tol' me I ha' to bring you closh." He looked up proudly, then dropped his eyes when he saw I was still

107

buttoning up my britches. "I foun' you, din' I? I foun' you aw by myshel'?"

"Yes, Elliot."

"Wuzzat good?"

"Yes, Elliot."

He was staring at me again, squinching his eyes against the dark, but I didn't object since I was nearly dressed. "Wha' happen?"

"What do you mean, 'wha' happen?' I lost my clothes. That's wha' happen."

"How?"

I don't know what made me say it. I swear I don't. I guess I was just exasperated and angry and—scared. Yes, that, too. "Some kidnappers got me."

"Wha'?"

"Kidnappers. They steal kids. They thought if they took my clothes away, I couldn't escape and run home."

His eyes were wide and wild now. He peered all around the icehouse in case the villains were lurking in the shadows. "Oh, Robbie." He breathed my name. "Tha's turrible."

"Yes," I said. "Terrible."

"Worse'n bein' los'."

"Yes," I agreed. "Because kidnappers don't care what they do to you, long as they get their money."

"Wha' money?"

"The ransom money. They make your family and friends pay lots of money to get you back safe."

"Oh, Robbie," he said in his little-boy voice. "But it's aw right now. I brung your closh. You can run 'way home."

"It ain't that easy, Elliot," I said sadly. "Ain't that easy."

"No?"

"No. You see, they got me hypnotized."

"Hippo—?"

"Hypnotized. It means they got control of my mind. It . . . well, it just ain't safe for me to go home right now."

"It ain'?" He gave another look around the icehouse. "Robbie," he whispered, "I scare'."

"Don't worry, Elliot. They don't have any hold over you. You just run along home and act like you don't know where I am or anything. Then they won't do nothing to you. But if you were to tell—well, I can't say what might happen if you tell."

"Not even Pa or Ma?"

"Nobody," I said. "Especially not Pa or Ma."

"Oh," he said. "I don' want da bad men to hur' you, Robbie."

"You needn't worry about me, Elliot. I'm a smart boy. I'll figure something out. You go along, now. And don't tell anyone you saw me, hear?"

"I won' tell, Robbie." He hesitated a few more seconds, then bolted out the door, leaving it wide open behind him.

Willerton's Digestive Remedy

After Elliot left, I closed the door. Once again the darkness nearly suffocated me. I felt my way around the wall to the stool. With britches on, I dared to sit down. What was I to do? I couldn't stay in the icehouse, even if I'd had a wish to. Elliot could hardly be trusted to keep my hiding place a secret for very long.

The cabin. Only Willie and I ever went there. Zeb and Vile were tramps. They'd probably swallowed their filthy stew and gone on their way by now. Jeezums crow, I hoped they had.

I made for the eastern hills. I felt safer running through the woods, at least until I was well on the other side of town. I came down from the woods a mile or so north of the town limits, still on the run.

Mostly, I was just running to keep from facing the music. If Mr. Weston had already "come calling," as Elliot said, then it wasn't a social visit. Pa, poor Pa. He tried so hard to help me get hold of my temper. It wasn't his fault I was such a hothead. But Mr. Weston would blame him, I felt sure. A preacher is supposed to keep his own children in line, clean and good, an example to other men's children. I was sure Willie had fled to keep from having to tell what he knew. Oh, drat it all.

Well, it wouldn't be any mystery to Pa why I hadn't come home for dinner or supper even, maybe. He'd reckon I was lying low for a spell. I figured it would be true dark before he started to worry. And as soon as he began to fret, Elliot would tell him I was in the icehouse, which he would believe, and that I'd been kidnapped, which he wouldn't (would he?). Anyhow, he wouldn't know to look for me at the cabin. That was Willie's and my secret, and Willie was no snitch.

If I stayed away long enough, everyone would forget how mad they were at me and take to fretting over my welfare. All I had to do was stay gone overnight, or at the most a couple of nights, and the whole town would organize a search. Even the Westons would forget how awful I had been and wonder if I was dead or lying out in the woods, calling faintly for help which never came.

Maybe, if I could stay out of sight long enough, they'd have a funeral for me, like they did for Tom Sawyer and Huck Finn. I'd like that. I'd like it even better if I could peek in on the proceedings and hear people say what a good fellow I was—just a little mischievous, as befitting a red-blooded American boy, but in reality a prince of a fellow, a credit, all things considered, to his grieving parents.

But what if they were still mad at Pa? For not believing enough in Hell and believing too much in monkeys? Well, if I was dead, they'd have to forgive him, a man who'd lost his only real son. Had he lost Elliot, they'd have said it was all for the best, like they do when any maimed or suffering creature dies. If he lost me, though, they'd talk about "lost promise" and "untimely demise" and "cut off before his prime"—that sort of pitiful phrase. Yes. It would truly elevate Pa's standing both in the community and the church if folks was to see him suffering a bit.

Would he cry for me? Would he? I mustn't think about that.

There's a wild raspberry patch growing alongside the tracks north of town. With all the sun we'd had that summer, the berries were already ripe. I stopped and stuffed my mouth with the sweet red fruit. I didn't even bother to pick off the little green bugs that like raspberries as much as I do. Now and then I got a bitter taste of one in a mouthful, but I didn't care. The berries took the warmth of the sun right to my cold belly. Or was it my cold heart?

If I'd had anything to carry berries in, I would have taken some with me to the cabin for later, but I didn't, so I just ate until my belly gave a warning pang that I had overdone it. Then, bellyache or no, I left the tracks, crossed the Tyler road, and forded the North Branch. I climbed the west hill a lot more cheerfully than I had come down the east.

There was no smoke curling up from the cabin's crumbling chimney, which I took to be a good sign—until I went inside. The iron kettle, complete with chicken bones, head, and feet, was still on the cold hearth, as was Zeb's ragged quilt. From the smell, I guessed it was the same old chicken I'd met the week before. There was no sign of either Zeb or Vile.

At least I'd have a chance to settle in. I went into the woods and broke off some pine boughs, stripped the branches off the tough limbs, and made myself a bed, as far away from Zeb's as I could get without moving under the broken part of the roof. I lay down to try it out. A pine-bough bed is not nearly as soft as it sounds in books. The needles poked my body and tickled and pricked my cheek. I rolled over on my back and pulled my shirt collar up to protect my neck. After a while, lying there listening to the birds and squirrels and the rustling of the breeze in the leaves, I fell asleep.

"What're you doing here?" Vile was leaning over me, a couple of small black-nosed dace dangling in front of my nose.

"You been using my pole," I said, secretly glad she'd caught nothing but dace with it.

She snorted. "Everything's yourn, ain't it?"

I sat up, pushing the fish out of my face. "Where's Zeb?"

"Mr. Finch to you."

I don't know why it surprised me that Zeb, and for

that matter Vile, had a last name. "Sure," I said. I wasn't adverse to calling Zeb "Mister." Hadn't I always been taught to respect my elders? Whatever else Zeb was or was not, he was my elder. "Where's *Mister* Finch?"

"No need to be sassy." There was obviously no way to get it right. She gave my pine-bough bed the once-over. "Made yourself right at home, I see."

"As a matter of fact—"

"Yeah, I know. You own it." She sighed and went over to the cooking pot, looked in, and gave a deeper sigh. Starting for the door, she tripped on Zeb's quilt and nearly fell. She gave the quilt a kick. "If you was really at home here, you wouldn't leave everything in such a mess."

I opened my mouth to protest but caught myself. I might have to be here as long as two days. I didn't fancy sleeping in the woods. "You want me to pitch that stuff out in the trees someplace?" I said, waving my hand at the pot.

"What? The chicken? No. We got to get a couple more days of soup out of that." A couple more days? My stomach lurched at the thought.

"I could make a fire," I said, getting up, tucking my shirt in.

She turned in the doorway to study me. "Since when did you get so helpful all of a sudden?"

I could feel my ears tingling. Tarnation. Couldn't I do anything without turning red all over?

"Here," she said, handing me her puny dace. "You do the fish."

I hate to clean fish. Especially small ones. There wouldn't be much left of these once the head, fins, and tail were gone. I reached out to take them, then remembered that my pocketknife was at the bottom of Cutter's Pond. "I—I must have forgot my knife again," I said.

She pulled the horn-handled jackknife out of her pocket and threw it at me. I made a try at catching it in my left hand and failed. She giggled.

Outside, we both set to work. Vile was getting wood for the fire. She had a pile of dead branches she must have dragged from the woods earlier in the day. She stepped on these and broke them into fireplace lengths. When she had an armful, she carried them into the cabin and came back to prepare more. I'd never seen a girl so handy at man's work. I guess she had to be or starve. Zeb didn't strike me as the industrious type. When she'd finished breaking up all the branches, she began to arrange the last bits teepee style for an outdoor fire.

Meantime, I'd found a flat rock where I could cut off the heads, fins, and tails of the little silvery fish. These I pitched into the woods. I scaled them best I could. The rock shone like it was set with slimy mica. Then I slit their bellies and pulled out the offal. My hands were slimy, too.

"Don't throw nothing away," she called to me without looking up from her work.

"Nothing?"

"Good for soup," she said.

I looked at the offal clinging to my hands. It wasn't going into any soup I was eating. I wiped myself as best I could on the dry leaves around the rock. Now bits of leaves stuck to the mess on my hands. I gave Vile the fish and went to the spring to wash.

She had the fire going and the dace browning on a green stick when Zeb came stumbling into sight. Vile straightened up from the fire and faced him accusingly. "You been at it again," she said.

"How could I," he asked pitifully, "when I ain't got a copper penny to my name?"

"I don't know how you manage it," she said. "But you been at the booze. No need to lie."

"Them leetle fish smell mighty good," he said.

"Oh, you're sweet, ain't you, now you got a little juice inside you?" She went back to her cooking, turning the fish until they were crisp. My mouth was fairly watering over those two tiny dace. Were we going to have to share them with the old drunkard, who hadn't done a lick of the work of catching or preparing?

"Go down to the spring and wash yourself up," she ordered him. "You look like a tramp."

His giggle was almost as girllike as her own. I thought he might protest, but he stumbled off in the direction of the spring.

"What am I going to do with him?" she asked, more to herself than to me.

When Zeb returned, his face was redder but no cleaner than it had been when he left, and his smell, if anything, was stronger. The three of us sat on the ground around the dying fire. Vile broke up the fish and portioned it out on three maple leaves. I couldn't help but think of the miracle in the Bible when Jesus fed five thousand with five loaves of bread and two small fish. Only this time there wasn't any miracle.

I tried to make my puny share last as long as I could. Even with no salt, the fish tasted fine, crisp and black on the outside and flaky inside. Zeb stuffed his portion into his mouth all at once, then looked around for more. Vile passed him her leaf with her last bite. He stuffed that in, too. White fish meat fell from his greedy lips to his shirt front. He fumbled to retrieve it, succeeding only in knocking it first to his trouser leg and then to the ground, where it was lost in the dead leaves on which we sat. I wanted to hit him for taking her food that way—not even spending the time to taste it proper, then wasting it in his drunken clumsiness.

When he realized there was nothing more to eat, he struggled to his feet and lumbered into the cabin. Before long we could hear his drunken snoring.

"You gave him your dinner," I whispered. I was a little in awe of Vile at that moment.

"He's my paw," she said. "How could I not?" I wanted to say, *Fathers are supposed to take care of their children, not the other way around.* She went into the cabin and reappeared with the cooking pot. "Where's the fish heads and things?" she asked.

"The heads?"

"I need them for the soup."

"I—I pitched them into the woods."

She sighed at the waste. "I reckon the coons had a feast," she said, then paused, a little embarrassed. "No way you can fetch us any more of those pitiful taters and carrots, is there?" She didn't wait for an answer, just sighed again and headed for the spring.

I busied myself gathering wood and twigs for the next fire. I didn't want her to think I was mooching off her. But I was, wasn't I? She'd caught two small fish, and I had gobbled down most of one of them. I was worse than her dratted pa. I wasn't even kin.

It was hours until suppertime—whatever supper could be made from rotting chicken head and feet—but I went ahead and laid a fire in the fireplace inside. Zeb was snorting and snoring. The smell of him was nauseous, so I worked fast and got out to the fresh air as soon as I could. Vile wasn't back yet. I imagined her squeezing the pot against the earth. Trying to force the spring to give up water would be worse than milking a dry cow. The North Branch was a long round trip, but in the end it might be easier. I planned to suggest it.

I wondered if I should go down to the tracks and pick some raspberries. I went back into the cabin and found two battered tin cups. They smelled of old soup. I shuddered.

They hadn't even been washed clean. I took them outside and wiped them as carefully as I could with maple leaves, but the grease just smeared around the inside. Cold water wouldn't help. It was the only time in my life that I felt a longing for the smell of good strong lye soap. How could you eat raspberries that had sat in old chicken grease?

You should never run away from home unprepared, believe me. I didn't have so much as my own tin cup, and I didn't fancy sharing one of theirs. I tiptoed past the smelly body of Zeb to replace the cups on the mantel. Zeb snorted and turned over. How had he gotten liquor? I knew, if you had money, there were ways, but Zeb was dirt poor. He didn't have any money, or did he? The old scalawag. It was all I could do to keep from rolling him over and going through his pockets.

At that moment I wanted more than anything to show him up. To make myself a hero and savior to Vile. *See,* I'd say. *You ain't so poor. Here's money. You can go down into town and buy you some proper grub.* But I didn't go through Zeb's pockets. I knew Vile'd never forgive me if I made a fool of her pa. She was like Willie—loyal to the core. I'd have to think of some better way to help her.

Zeb was still asleep when Vile got back. "Might as well start the fire," she said. "It'll take eternity to make soup from this."

If she was grateful for my laying the fire, she didn't say so. Just took one of the big lucifer matches Willie and

I had left on the mantel and struck it, lighting the kindling. I held my breath. I didn't want Vile to despise me for not being able to lay a proper fire. I watched the flames leap from the dried leaves and twigs, dance around the loose bark, and then envelop the larger branches.

Relieved, I went outside, leaving Vile to put the pot on to boil. When she came out, she was livid with rage. She waved a bottle at me. "Looka here!" she cried. "Can you beat this?"

The half-filled bottle she held out for my inspection was Willerton's Digestive Remedy. The drugstore sells gallons of it. Half the town, mostly the male half, fancies it has digestive problems that only Willerton's can ease. "He musta had a bellyache," I said lamely.

"Bellyache, my big toe!" She loosened the cap and jammed the bottle under my nose. "Just smell that."

"Smells like Willerton's to me," I said, my eyes smarting from the fumes. "Stomach remedies gotta be strong to work."

"You *are* a newborn babe, ain't you? Willerton's is nothing but booze with a fancy name. How you think he got drunk as a skunk?" She hauled back and threw the bottle straight and hard as a strike over the plate, crashing it against the rough bark of a nearby spruce. The liquid made a dark stain against the trunk. Then she did something that surprised me more than I can say. She sat down cross-legged on the ground, put her head in her hands, and burst out crying.

I didn't know what to say or do. I called her name softlike a couple of times, but she paid me no mind. She was not going to be comforted by gentle words. I needed something more powerful than Willerton's to soothe her ills. That was when I came up with my brilliant idea.

Lord, deliver me from my brilliant ideas. But at the time, on a nearly empty stomach, with Vile crying her eyes out, it seemed born of pure genius.

My Brilliant Scheme

The two of us were sitting outside, leaning against the side of the cabin. Vile was staring glumly at the ashes of our dinnertime fire. Through the wall I could hear Zeb snoring away like a bear in hibernation. It was time, I thought, to tell her.

"Vile," I said, "I've got an idea."

She sniffed and turned to look at me, one eyebrow raised.

"No, really. I got an easy way for us to make money."

"Yeah?" Ha! I'd figured the word *money* would make her sit up and take notice.

"We write a ransom note, see?"

"A what?"

I stopped to explain to her about the Clark baby and the New York boy and how it happened all the time. She was still giving me her puzzled expression.

"See, we pretend I got kidnapped and ask for money to get me back—"

"Who would pay good money—?"

"Just listen, Vile. People do it. They take up a collection. All we got to do is write the note. First they collect the money and put it in the secret place we told them to in the note. Next, you and I sneak down and get it and divide it up. Then you and Zeb skedaddle out of the county and I walk down the hill and appear on Main Street, sort of half dazed. I may have amnesia"—the look on her face made me hurry to explain—"can't remember anything about what happened to me, but since I've returned unharmed otherwise, everybody's happy."

"Especially the sheriff who's on Paw's and my tail."

"What sheriff?" I asked, and then was immediately sorry I had. Her look was enough to sizzle a sausage.

"You was talking about—"

"Yeah. My amnesia. See. For weeks I can't remember anything. Then, finally, after you and Zeb is well out of Vermont, little by little I start to recall stuff. But when I do, the kidnappers don't look anything like you two."

"Yeah? And who's going to believe you?"

"Oh, they won't doubt me. I'm the preacher's boy. Besides, I'm the only witness as well as the victim. They'll believe me, all right."

"No."

"No what?"

"Just no. I don't want no part of such a fool plan."

"I'm thinking we should ask for one thousand dollars—two might seem a bit greedy."

Out of the corner of my eye I could see new interest

flickering up. "Your paw got that kind of money?"

"Oh, no. He's a preacher. But that's just what will make everyone feel sorry and want to help. The town will raise it, you see. Just like they did in New York when Marion Clark disappeared in the arms of her nurse. The banks, the stores, everybody will pitch in."

"But you ain't some darling little baby—"

"C'mon, Vile, they'd do it for any child in town that got lost." I was arguing with myself as well as Vile. Surely they'd do it for me. Didn't the whole town turn out when the Wilson baby wandered out on Cutter's Pond and the ice was about to break up? They risked their lives, laying a human chain across the ice to her. Course, she was a darling three-year-old with yellow curls, not some rapscallion of a boy. I looked over at Vile. She wasn't watching my face for self-doubts; she was counting the cash in her mind.

"You ask for it in small bills," I went on. "I mean, sure, if you was to show up in Tyler or even Montpelier, throwing hundred-dollar bills around—"

"They got hundred-dollar bills?"

"Sure," I said. Though I'd never actually seen one, I knew for a fact there was such a thing.

"There's some piece of paper that's worth one hundred dollars?"

"It takes ten of them to make a thousand," I said, in case her arithmetic was weak. "But you wouldn't want hundred-dollar bills. They'd look suspicious if you tried to spend one in a store."

She looked disappointed. I think she liked the idea of holding a fistful of hundred-dollar bills.

"And there's no chance we'll get caught?"

"None a-tall. They leave the money whatever place we tell them to. We already warned them that we'll kill the victim if they try to watch for us or call in the sheriff. Like I said, after we divide it, I give you and Zeb—Mr. Finch—a day's start, then I let myself be discovered wandering down Main Street in a daze. A couple of weeks later I dimly recalls these—uh—hoboes with great black beards who took me captive and threatened my life."

She gave a short laugh, picturing herself, I suppose, as a black-bearded hobo. Then she sobered. "Do we have to tell Paw about it?"

"Well, he'll sort of be in on it."

"Yeah, but if he knows about the plan, he'll turn all funny. Especially when he's liquored up. He might even brag."

"We can't have that!"

"No, we can't. So it'll have to be jest between us two, okay, Ed?"

"Okay." I'd given up reminding her that my name was supposed to be Fred.

After much thought I decided it would be fitting to write the note with a chicken quill dipped in berry juice the color of blood. Unfortunately, raspberries was the only thing I was sure was ripe. I didn't know how raspberry ink would work, but I sent Vile down to the patch with her tin cup to get some. We couldn't risk anyone seeing me down there. Using birch bark for paper would be a nice touch, but the Finches had all that paper tied up in the kerchief, so why not use it? Besides, only Indians would think to use birch bark. Hoboes, I figured, were more likely to use the backs of Wanted posters. I wondered if Zeb's picture was on one of those posters, but I wasn't sure I had the nerve to ask.

It seemed to take Vile forever. The more I thought of the chicken quill and berry ink, the less I liked the idea. I longed for the pencil stub that along with my pocketknife was at the bottom of Cutter's Pond. And that wasn't all. There was my taw (I'd never be able to shoot a decent game of marbles without it), a ragged handkerchief (my ma often checked to make sure I had one on me), even a few pennies, in case I was seized with pangs of uncontrollable hunger just as I was passing the general store and had to have a sourball or lemon stick. Darn it all.

I wondered if they were missing me yet. I sighed. Pa wouldn't start looking for me while it was still daylight. Then I remembered it was Wednesday. He wouldn't start looking for me until after prayer meeting was done. I told myself that was a good thing. It would give me lots of time to work out the scheme.

I squinted up at the sun. I made it to be no later than four in the afternoon. I shouldn't have thought about sourballs. I was seized with pangs of hunger unlike any I had ever experienced before. My belly had let those few bites of dace go past without hardly noticing. I tried not to smell the pot bubbling in the cabin, which I felt sure my gut would reject altogether.

I wondered what Mr. Weston had said to Pa, and what Pa had said back. Did Pa take up my side? If I'd been a Filipino, he would have. But how could he defend me? He knew the kind of temper I had. He was not likely to doubt that I had indeed tried to drown Ned Weston, or at least scare the devil out of him.

For a fellow who'd given up on God and the Ten Commandments, I was feeling myself strangely close to what Reverend Pelham would have called a vile sinner. I recalled the awful rage that had come over me, making me shove Ned Weston's head under the water. Willie thought I was fixing to kill Ned. He was right. I might have. I really might have. I felt sick all over just remembering it.

Then it occurred to me that it was really Pa's fault—not altogether, not even mostly, but surely a little bit. He had no business having those heathen books around where anybody, especially some pious deacon or hell-fire reverend, could just wander in and see them sitting bold as brass on the shelf. Like Reverend Pelham said, Pa was a preacher. He owed it to God not to go flirting with the powers of evil and unbelief, now, didn't he? Surely Pa didn't think people descended from apes, no matter what trashy books he had sitting around.

But ever since the night Elliot was lost, I was thinking worrisome thoughts about Pa. Why did that crying over Elliot get to me so? Was he having some kind of nervous disorder? If so, what would my disappearance do to him? Or, for that matter, his knowing that his son was a near murderer? Would that do him in?

Yes, it would be better for him to think I was kidnapped than to think I was a fugitive from the law. Wouldn't it? I was banking heavy on Mr. Weston coming to feel sorry I was gone and forgetting all about my attacking his boy. What if, even after I was miraculously returned to the bosom of my family, Mr. Weston still hadn't forgiven and forgotten? Then Pa would get it with both barrels—his son the victim of a vicious crime *and* his son the perpetrator, or near perpetrator, of an equally heinous crime, one against the son of the town's most important citizen. Oh, mercy.

Along about then, Vile trudged up the hill into sight. "Birds got most of your berries," she said. I couldn't help but notice that her mouth was stained light purple. She held out the cup. It was about half full. I got a stick and smashed the berries into a pulpy juice. Vile fetched me a handbill from the kerchief in the cabin. It had a sketch on the front of a bank robber in Albany. I restrained myself from asking questions about robbers *or* what she and Zeb had been doing in New York State. Avoiding as best I could the fish mess on the flat rock, I set to work.

Have you ever tried to write anything with a chicken-feather quill? I swear, I don't know how Thomas Jefferson could possibly have got through anything the length of the Declaration of Independence with just a quill pen. Of course, he had a proper desk and real ink. In about ten minutes I had only managed, in pale wobbly letters, to write "Help!"

Vile was leaning over my shoulder, bumping my right arm to make matters worse. "Awful weak," she said. "I can't hardly read it."

"I can't help it," I said. "Raspberries ain't good ink." I had planned to write out "Help! I have been kidnapped!" But after all that trouble with "Help!" I just put "Kidnapped!" next. I still had to write all that stuff about the ransom—where and when.

"I don't think it's going to work," she said.

"You're right," I said finally. "But where are we going to get proper pen and ink? Or even a lead pencil?"

She put her hands on her hips, thinking. "Hmm. Why don't we go down tonight to the general store and help ourselves to one?"

"'Cause if we're caught, the jig is up."

"We wouldn't get caught. Leastways, *I* wouldn't."

I didn't ask her why she was so sure. I didn't really want to know all Vile's experiences with breaking the law. "If we were to get caught—and you got to allow the possibility, Vile, that something might go wrong—if we did get caught, not only would we lose any chance of getting the ransom money, we'd both be thrown into jail."

"What jail? You can't tell me this one-horse town's got a jail."

"Yes, we do," I said in a dignified way as befit a loyal citizen. "In the town hall basement. It's not big. It's, well, it's more like a circus cage—"

"A cage?" She drew back, horrified. "They put people in a cage like some wild beast?"

I nodded solemnly. I had actually never seen anyone in the cage, but I had often seen the cage—all iron bars— in the town hall basement.

"Wal, I guess that puts the lid on your big scheme, then."

I wasn't quite ready to give it up. It was prayer-meeting night at both the Congregational and Methodist churches. A good night for a minor burglary. I could burgle the manse while everyone was down at church. There'd be no one around to catch me, and even if someone did, it wasn't likely that they'd call the sheriff to arrest me for robbing my own house. And I could pick up some foodstuff while I was at it. Vile liked that idea fine. All we had to do was wait until prayer-meeting time and hope our stomachs didn't cave in before then.

Vile dug the rest of the raspberry "ink" out of her cup and slurped it up. Then she went in and dipped out some of her soup into both the cups. She handed me Zeb's. It seemed unmannerly not to take it, though you can just imagine how anxious I was to drink *that* soup out of a cup belonging to *that* man.

Let me tell you, I have tasted some bilious potions in my time, but nothing quite to beat that single sip of Vile's antique chicken-head soup. It was all I could do not to throw up my guts.

She was watching me anxiously. "It ain't my best effort," she said apologetically.

"It's fine," I said, coughing and covering my mouth. "I'm just not very hungry, that's all." I couldn't imagine even God (if there was a God) would blame a person for lying under those circumstances.

We sat there, our backs against the side of the cabin, she drinking, me pretending to drink the soup. We were so quiet that we could hear the late-afternoon breeze stirring the leaves and the lazy chirping of the birds. The insects were down to a low hum. It was peaceful in the woods. Even the sound of Zeb's snoring was muffled by the log wall. Then it stopped. We could hear him shudder to his feet and begin rattling around the cabin.

Suddenly, a roar of "Viiiiile!" I froze, and beside me I felt Vile do the same.

"Paw," she whispered.

He came thundering out the door. Before this I'd only seen him as a sort of stupid old man, but Zeb was transformed. His eyes were blazing, his mouth wide showing all his rotting teeth. He looked seven feet tall, waving his arms about and bellowing, "Where is it? Which of you varmints stole my bottle? I'll kill the bustard!"

Among the Stones

Vile and I were both on our feet. As I jumped up, Zeb's tin cup bounced to the ground splattering greasy soup on my bare feet and the bottom of my britches legs.

"Where's m' bottle, I say!" Neither Vile nor I made a sound; we just stood there backed against the wall.

Zeb lunged for Vile, grabbed her by her thin shoulders, and shook her like a cat shakes its quarry before it kills it. "Don't play dumb with me, girl. I know you got it!"

She's a brave one, that Vile. She kept her lips clamped together. Not a sound came out, even when he left off shaking her and smacked her hard across the face with his right hand.

That old familiar rage came boiling up. How dare he hurt her? The knife was still lying by the rock. I grabbed it. "Let her go!" I cried, raising it like a dagger.

"Stay out of this, Ed," she said through her teeth, not turning around, but Zeb could see the knife. More in surprise than anything else, he loosed his grip. Vile shook herself and backed up slowly, putting the flat stone between herself and her father.

He glanced down at the stone. My failed attempt to write a ransom note still lay there. He squinted at it. I prayed he couldn't read. But he obviously could make out the first word.

"What's this now?" He snatched up the paper. "Help?" He glared at us both. "Jest who needs help around here?" His tone was threatening, but I knew he was keeping the knife in view. He didn't move toward either of us.

"Jest a game, Paw. No harm meant."

"I don't fancy your games, girl," he said, jamming the "Help! Kidnapped!" note into his pocket. He shot another glance at the knife.

Vile turned toward me to see what he was looking at. "Put down the knife, Ed," she said. "He ain't gonna hurt you."

"Jest tell me where m' bottle got to. That's all I'm after." But even as he spoke, he saw the broken glass under the spruce tree and the dark stain on its trunk.

"Why, you leetle—" He made as if to lunge for her, but I was quicker this time, jumping toward him, the rusty blade high. He stopped with a jerk.

The knife shook in my hand. He'd soon see I was bluffing. "Run, Vile," I said. She hesitated. "Run!" I yelled it this time. "I'll catch up." I started to run, snapping the knife into its handle as I did. Zeb came after me. I turned and hurled the folded knife at him. I heard him yelp, so I must have hit the target, but I wasn't waiting around to see. I was chasing through the brush down the hill as fast as I could tear. I soon caught up with Vile, grabbed her hand, and pulled her along, the branches scraping our faces and bodies as we stumbled on.

"You didn't hurt him?" she managed to pant out.

"No. Promise. Just keep going. He's after us." I could hear his clumsy thrashing on the hillside above us. "C'mon. Faster." Still holding her hand, I headed diagonally north down the hill. I was banking on Zeb to follow the path straight down toward the center of town.

At last we were at the creek. I realized suddenly that I was still holding her hand. I dropped it quickly. Vile pretended not to notice, just stood there holding her side and panting for a minute. "We'd better keep going," I said, wading straight in. I guess I was figuring my feet and britches would welcome a rinse after their chicken-head soup shower. Vile nodded and followed after, surprising me by lifting her tattered hem up about ten inches, holding her skirts as dainty as if she was a member of the Ladies' Aid Society. She'd got her voice back after the race down the hill. "Where we headed?" she asked.

"To the stone sheds. We can rest there a bit—decide what to do next." I didn't want to use the word *hide*. I was afraid she might balk at the idea. Still, she looked worried. "They let off work at three. Nobody will be around."

"How we going to get in?"

"They don't lock up. Who's going to steal granite? You need a crane to move it at all, and a train or at least a team of horses to carry it away."

After I'd made sure there was nothing coming from either direction, we crossed the Tyler road, then the railroad tracks. Each of us pulled a few berries as we went past the raspberry patch, but we did it on the move. I figured we'd do what I'd done earlier, hike up to the woods and go south toward the stone sheds under the cover of the trees. Once we were near the backs of the sheds, we could drop down the hill and sneak into one of them.

"Ed," she said, "we shouldn'ta left him."

"What?" I couldn't believe my ears.

"He ain't got no more sense than a toadstool when he goes off his head like this."

"Nothing going to happen to *him*," I said firmly. The picture of Zeb shaking and slapping Vile was burned into my mind. It was hard to believe she was worried about him.

"It's the booze, you know. He's a good sort, really. Don't mean no harm."

I looked at the red spot on her cheekbone. "Well, he may not have meant to, but that rosebud on your face is going to bloom into a beauty of a shiner."

She patted her cheek gently. "It don't hurt none."

"Maybe not," I said. "But let's just wait out this crazy spell, okay?"

She didn't argue, just kept following me. We came down behind the first shed. The back door opened easily. There was still dust in the air of the shed, giving it a twilight feel. Inside, large blocks of still-raw granite were mixed with tombstones in various stages of progress.

"I don't like it," Vile whispered. "It's like a graveyard."

"It's just granite," I said. "Stone. There ain't no bodies buried here."

"I'm saying what it *feels* like," she said in a more normal tone of voice.

I sat down on a rectangular block that was resting benchlike on one side. I patted the place beside me. "Might as well rest."

She obeyed, perching on the edge of the granite. After a while she got up and began to pace among the stones. I felt too tired to stand up, much less walk, though the cold of the stone was penetrating, especially where my pants legs were damp.

She came back to where I sat. "I need to go look for him," she said.

"He won't thank you," I said. "He's likely still mad about the bottle."

"I shouldn'ta done it," she said. "It's his only comfort." I couldn't believe she'd defend him and said as much. "He can't help it, Ed. It's like a sickness."

I grunted. "More like demon possession."

"You don't understand. You're a preacher's boy."

136

"I've heard plenty about the demon rum," I said. And I had. Leonardstown had a very active chapter of the Temperance Union. They'd even brought traveling theatrical companies to town, who acted out melodramas about the evils of drink. In fact, if at that very moment one of those pious ladies had magically appeared, pledge card in hand, I think I would have signed it, swearing off intoxicating spirits for the rest of my natural life. I'd had too vivid a sample in the last hour of what alcohol could do, and it made me furious as well as scared.

She wandered off again, leaving me to ponder the evils of drink. "Hey!" she called a few minutes later. "Look what I found." She came around a stone angel at the far end of the row, carrying what looked like a lunch pail. "Somebody forgot to eat their dinner."

She put it down on the stone and lifted the lid. It was a feast—bread, cheese, even a large slab of pie, which when unwrapped proved to be raspberry. "It's a miracle," I said, "just when we were about to starve." She looked at me oddly. I didn't try to explain that if God provided a miracle, then it couldn't be considered stealing to accept it. And even if, strictly speaking, it was stealing to eat somebody else's dinner that they'd forgotten to eat earlier, well, I didn't have to worry anyway, being currently an unbeliever. It was too complicated to explain to her.

Vile smoothed out a piece of the paper wrapping and spread the feast out on the granite. "There's even something to drink," she said, taking a corked green glass bottle out of the pail. She yanked out the cork, smelled the contents, then handed the bottle across to me.

I sniffed. It was some stonecutter's homemade—there was no mistaking it. "It's wine," I said.

"Oh," she said, replacing the cork. "Then I'll save it for Paw."

"Are you out of your mind, Vile?"

She sighed. "I guess I won't." She put the bottle back into the pail. "Here," she said in a more cheerful voice, breaking the longish loaf of bread in two and then the cheese. "Let's eat."

The bread was crusty on the outside and a little bit hard, as was the cheese, but it didn't matter to either of us. By the time we had worked our way to the pie, we were full enough to eat more slowly, rolling every bite around in our mouths to get the last bit of flavor.

"I bet the president of the Yu-nited States don't eat this good," she said, smacking her lips, which were now more stained with raspberry juice than before.

"Probably not," I agreed, knowing in fact that in the white manse on School Street we ate like this on many an ordinary day, but I had never been truly hungry before. It does add something powerfully delicious to a meal to eat it when you're so hungry.

When we had pinched every crumb from the wrapping papers, she gave another tremendous sigh. "We didn't save Paw a bite," she said. I could see her eyeing that little bottle of wine.

"No, Vile," I said. "You give that to Zeb, you'll only be sorry after."

The bell in the Congregational church steeple rang, calling the faithful to prayer meeting. Just the time we'd planned to steal the pencil, but the great scheme no longer seemed so promising.

"Now what?" Vile asked, just as I was wondering myself. She folded the papers neatly and put them into the pail. "Let's go back to the cabin and get some sleep," she said. "By this time he'll be meek as a lamb—you'll see."

Vile ran ahead of me the last hundred yards or so and got to the cabin first. "He's not here," she said as I walked up.

"No?" I said, trying, for her sake to sound disappointed. I'd been banking heavy on his not being there, else I'd never have agreed to return.

"We got to find him," she said. "No telling what trouble he's liable to get himself into, state he's in."

I hope you won't write me off for a coward when I tell you how little I wanted to go back down that hill. I just wanted to lie on my scratchy pine-bough bed with my full, happy stomach and go to sleep. But how was I going to let her go looking for him alone? Meek as a lamb, huh? The man was as liable to kill her as not. "In the dark?" I asked, for the summer dusk was fast fading into night.

She was determined, so I said we should take the path to Webster's pasture. That way we could make it down without losing our way in the dark. My head was as heavy as my feet. "Wait up," I called to Vile, who was bouncing ahead of me despite the night closing in. "You'll miss the path at that rate." She waited for me to catch up.

"I know it's bad for him, but I can't help wishing I'd brought that wine."

"Don't even think of such a thing!" The girl had no sense sometimes. "It's like poison to him."

"I know," she said sadly. "But at first he's happy. I like to see him happy."

"Just don't forget afterward, when he gets mean and stupid. Just keep that picture in your head."

She left me again and moments later tripped over a root or something, pitching forward. I pulled her to her feet. "Not so fast, Vile. You can't even see your feet. You'll just get hurt if you try to run."

She stayed close after that. There was only the fingernail of a moon, and it was not much use. I was grateful for the well-worn path.

It was about then that I saw the bobbing light. I put my hand on Vile's shoulder. We stopped dead and listened. Somebody was coming our way.

"Who can that be?" Vile whispered.

"Shh," I said. "I don't know." But in my heart I did know. Somehow, while we were running up and down the hill, prayer meeting had come and gone. The light was Pa, come looking for me. Part of me wanted to rush right for that light and throw myself into his arms. But the other, baser part, held back. If he found me now, I'd have hardly given him more worry than Elliot.

"Do you think they're after Zeb?" she whispered anxiously.

"Maybe. Better cut off into the woods until they get by. We don't want them asking us questions."

"No."

Waiting silently in the woods, I could hear what sounded like at least two people heading past us up the hill. They weren't talking. Perhaps they were trying to be quiet. To surprise me. There was only one reason Pa would be climbing the path to the cabin. Willie, my loyal Willie, had betrayed me.

I stood there in the darkness watching the light come up. When it came even to where we stood, I looked away. I didn't want to take a chance of glimpsing Pa's face in the lantern light. We waited until their footsteps were well out of earshot, then found the path and made our way down the hill. At the edge of the woods we moved northward till we were on a line to the sheds. There was a single light pole in the midst of the shed area, the lantern on top lit by gas, so we made for it. I longed to sneak into one of the sheds and spend the night, but Vile didn't stop. We took the route behind the sheds, staying off Main Street.

We snuck through the back yards of the houses between Depot Street and East Hill Road. Off East Hill Road is Prospect Street, where all the people in town who have the prospect of being rich build their houses. The Westons' is the biggest one up there.

I glanced up that direction a little nervously as we crossed East Hill Road, but I didn't have time to worry overmuch about the Westons coming after me. Vile was already grabbing my arm and pulling me toward the back of Wolcott's Drugstore. "Look!" she said. The back door had been battered in. "Hear that?"

Somebody or something was thrashing around inside. Once a poorly trained horse had broken out of the livery stable and galloped up the street through the open door of the meat market. It took half the town either yelling or grabbing to get it out of there. My first thought was that some such thing had happened again—this time in the drugstore. That's what all that crashing of glass and splintering of wood sounded like—a wild horse kicking and rearing at the display cases.

"It's Paw," Vile said. "He's got the blind crazies."

My first impulse, I'm ashamed to say, was to run as fast as possible in the opposite direction. It wasn't altogether yeller-belly—more like common sense. Vile, of course, marched right across the broken-down door like Daniel into the lions' den.

"Vile! Don't be stupid!" She didn't even turn her head. So what could I do? I might have given up being a Christian, but I had not yet given up on being a man. I followed that foolish girl through the storage room into the store itself.

That horse from the livery stable had done less damage than Zeb was doing in Wolcott's Drugstore, a place usually as neat as your grandma's needle case. He was roaring about, thrashing his limbs every which way, taking an entire shelf of bottles down with a single sweep of his big arm.

"Paw!" Vile called to him. "Paw! It's all right. I'm here now. Take it easy. C'mon, Paw, calm yourself down. Please, Paw—" She went closer and closer to him, speaking as gentle as a farmer to a ranting bull.

At first he didn't seem to hear or see her, but when she was a foot or so away, he turned with a roar, grabbing her by her hair. It looked as though he was going to twirl her around his head like that poor chicken. I sprang at his legs, knocking us all to the floor.

Vile jumped up. "C'mon, Ed!" she cried out, heading for the back door. But I got up a little too slowly. Zeb reached out from where he lay and grabbed a bottle from the floor. Before I could move, he brought it crashing down on my head.

The blow stunned us both. I could see his eyes go wide as he dropped the broken-off neck. Then I felt the cold liquid from the bottle mixing with something warmer. My head began to spin. I swear I saw fireworks right there in Wolcott's Drugstore.

Vile was yanking at my arm. I stumbled across Zeb's legs to my own wobbly feet. I was faintly aware that Zeb was not moving at all, just sitting there in the middle of the mess, looking stupid. I let Vile drag me outside the drugstore. She pulled me across the back yards and back toward the stone sheds. I was dizzy as a top, but somehow she kept me moving until we reached the nearest shed. As soon as she had managed to get me inside and close the door, I fainted dead away like Mabel Cramm on Decoration Day.

Thou Shalt Not Bear False Witness

Now, what follows next mostly took place when I was not in my right mind, so I have pieced it together from a variety of sources, some more reliable than others. If you suspect that some of my own overwrought imagination has managed to slip in and dress up the naked facts, well, that's a risk you're going to have to take.

Someone, probably someone who lived in one of the houses on North Main Street, heard the commotion inside Wolcott's Drugstore. Since they were well aware that nobody should have been there at ten o'clock of an evening, well past the bedtime of any Christian citizen, they decided not to investigate on their own but to send somebody else all the way to Wolcott's house on the south end of Prospect Street to tell him to come down and see what was making such an infernal racket on his business premises at such an ungodly hour. Mr. Wolcott, being on the stout and elderly side, thought that it would be more prudent to send his hired girl to go fetch the sheriff, who thought it wise to wake up two or three townsfolk and deputize them hastily. He didn't fancy marching into the ruckus and finding himself outnumbered.

At any rate, by the time the posse got there to investigate, what they found was a strange man of highly disreputable appearance snoring away on the drugstore floor surrounded by lots of glass and splintered wood, and a bit of blood. They thought at first that the blood was the vandal's own, but after they had got him on his feet and looked him over closely, they were forced to conclude that the man had no wounds to account for the blood on the floor. You can imagine the scene as the sheriff and his deputies hoisted Zeb to his feet and pretty much carried him to the town hall to lock him up—Zeb, bigger than any one of them, hollering and protesting and dragging his feet all the way down Main Street and up the town hall stairs and down the inside steps to the basement cage. The lock was rusty with disuse, the men exhausted. No one wanted to spend the night watching the prisoner, so the poor sheriff was forced to. He'd never bargained for a real crime when he'd run for office fifteen years before. It was hardly fair—a summons in the middle of the night, a repulsive stranger asleep amidst destruction, mysterious bloodstains—who did the town think they'd elected, anyway? That Sherlock Holmes feller?

Meantime the source of those mysterious bloodstains was lying out on the floor of the nearest stone shed, spurting rivers of scarlet. Vile tore off the hem of her none-too-clean dress, trying like crazy to stanch the flow. But to no avail. By this time half the town was awake and in the streets, trying to find out what all the carrying-on was about.

Vile, now near desperate to save what she thought of as my rapidly expiring life, gave up mopping my skull and ran out onto Main Street, grabbed the first person she saw, and made him come back with her to where I lay. You'll think I am making up this part, but the man she seized upon was none other than Mr. Earl Weston.

It was a stroke of luck for me, I tell you. By the time he'd carried my near lifeless body all the way up West Hill Road and down School Street to the manse, he was covered with my blood and panting like a dying horse. Why, he felt like a hero of the Great War who's carried his wounded comrade to safety. He'd hardly walked that far since he started wearing long pants, and he'd never delivered a bleeding child to the arms of its distraught mother. Ma told him what a wonderful godsend he was, and he believed her. He couldn't hate me after that. It's hard to be too harsh on someone when you think God has personally chosen you to save his life. He wasn't going to spoil his run as local hero and angel of God by demanding a pound of flesh out of my behind once I was vertical again.

Mr. Weston laid me down on the daybed in the kitchen, and Dr. Blake was summoned. I have a vague recollection of Dr. Blake picking glass out of my scalp with a long pair of tweezers, but I kept fainting away, so I cannot tell you to this day if, when Pa got home and saw me lying there, he cried to know that I was found.

At first the news seemed good. Dr. Blake got the glass out and stitched up my scalp. My skull—as Beth had always suspected—being harder than ordinary, had not been cracked by the blow. I was due for headaches for the next few days, Dr. Blake declared, but I was bound to recover. They hadn't reckoned on the infection. My fever zoomed so high that I was out of my head just as much as I would have been if my brain had been injured. All in all, I was hardly in this world for the next five days. Sometimes I knew someone, usually Ma, was wiping my forehead with a cool cloth or ladling broth into my mouth. Willie came by, but they wouldn't let him see me. What I remember best was Elliot leaning over me, patting me gently with a wet rag and singing softly, "Shall we gazur at da ri-ber?"

That, if nothing else, made me sure I was going to die. The idea of dying, regardless of whether or not I was one of the chosen gathering at the river, was just too awful. I decided then and there to fool them all and get well. That was the last time anybody had to sit by the daybed through the night to make sure I didn't die all alone.

As soon as I was pronounced to be in my right mind, I had a visit from the sheriff. He was very quiet and respectful, as is appropriate when one is addressing a person just returned from the banks of the River of Death. He apologized humbly, but he did have to ask me about the criminal currently locked up in the town hall jail. "Was he the one done this to you?" he asked, waving his hand at my bandaged head.

"Yessir," I said, weakly. It wouldn't have been polite to sound too robust under the circumstances.

"And this"—he produced a folded paper from his pocket, revealing my failed attempt to inaugurate my brilliant scheme—"is this your handwriting?"

I had to admit it was, though I felt ashamed to do so. What a childish idea it had been.

"Thank you, Robbie," he said, bobbing his head politely. "I won't trouble you further. You jest get all well now, you hear?"

"Thank you, sir," I said, my head still a bit muddled, wondering how the foolish ransom note had got mixed up in the affair.

I was soon to be enlightened. That night I was sleeping peacefully, fever-free and pretty much pain-free for the first time in days, only to be roughly awakened by someone shaking me furiously and a familiar hoarse whisper. "Ed, Ed, wake up. I got to talk to you."

There was Vile, one eye purple and green, leaning over the daybed. I must confess, in the closed air of the manse, the odor surrounding her was even more pungent than it seemed to be in the great outdoors.

"Vile," I said, trying to rouse up to my elbows.

"What are you doing here?" In the dim light I could see her face fall.

"I know I got no right here, but where could I turn?" Her whisper was high-pitched and frantic. "They got Paw. They're hauling him down to Tyler tomorrow." She made a sound that I would have called a sob if anyone else had made it. "They—they're like to hang him."

"Don't worry, Vile. They don't hang people for busting up stores."

"It ain't the store, Ed. They got it in their heads he kidnapped you and then tried to murder you."

"Why would they think that?" You're asking yourself why a boy as smart as me could be so totally ignorant, but remember, I had had a head wound *and* a high fever. My poor mind wasn't ticking as well as a cheap pocket watch about then.

"The runsum note," she said, her brow all furrowed. "Remember? Paw stuffed it in his pocket. They find the raspberry-juice note in his pocket. Then they find you with your head bashed in." She sighed. "It don't look too good. You can't hardly blame them."

"Oh," I said, easing myself to the pillow, remembering the sheriff's visit. Now to be perfectly honest, I knew that if the county judge decided to put Zeb in prison for the rest of his natural life, I would hardly be one to shed a teardrop, but hanging—even with my head like tapioca pudding, I could not rejoice to see any man on the gallows. It's not my fault. Pa has made me soft that way.

I guess my lying there not saying anything was making Vile nervous. She started sort of jumping from one foot to the other. "Ed, *please,* you got to do something. You know he didn't kidnap you."

"He whapped me on the head right proper," I said.

"I know, and he shouldn'ta done it, but you *did* pervoke him, Ed. It was partly your fault, innerfurrin' like you did."

All my sympathy flowed away like a spring torrent. I had "innerfurred" to save her dirty little neck. "Even if he didn't kidnap me, he *did* assault me, thereby committing bodily harm," I said primly. She opened her mouth to object. "He might have killed us both, Vile. You know that."

"He wouldn'ta *meant* to." She was pleading with me. "He would have felt sorry as a—a—sorry as could be afterwards. He really would've."

"Afterwards? There'd be no afterwards for you and me whether he meant it or not. That 'sorry' wouldn't count for an ice chip in Hades after we was dead and planted under the grass."

"Oh, Ed, please. *Please.* Think of your old pal Vile if you won't think of him. Paw's all I got in this world, Ed."

Suddenly it irritated me something awful for her to call me Ed. I know. I know. It doesn't make any sense. Who had started it all, trying to get them to think my name was Fred? But I was sick of Fred and Ed and Zeb and that awful cabin smelling of decaying chicken head and fish offal and wretched human sweat. I was even sick of having to worry about Vile.

I'm ashamed to say this, but I closed my eyes, hoping she would get the hint and leave. Before you judge me too harshly, remember how much glass was picked out of my scalp—how high my fever had shot to.

"Ed?" she said softly. "Please, Ed, before it's too late—"

I opened my eyes again. She looked so pitiful with that multicolored eye. What was to become of her? Where could she go? Back to that empty cabin where there was nothing to eat, the matches nearly used up? Before I could say anything, there was a sound on the stairs. She started like a doe. "Please," she said one more time before she dashed out the door.

Pa came into the kitchen. He pulled the quilt up close to my chin. "Are you awake, Robbie?" he asked softly. I kept my eyes closed while I tried to figure out what to answer. "Just talking in your sleep again?" He felt my forehead, seemed satisfied that my fever had not returned, then tiptoed out of the kitchen and back up the stairs.

You'd think an uneasy conscience would keep a person awake, but next thing I knew, the light was streaming through the windows and Ma was stirring up the breakfast fire. I sat up slowly so as to not rattle my head. Ma is a good-looking woman even from the back. She has long auburn hair tucked into a big bun on the top of her head, but she is always in a hurry, so short curly hairs escape and make a kind of halo around her face. I got her curly hair, but mine's more red than auburn. She says my Scottish grandpa gave it to me, but I wish he'd kept it to himself. In the modern United States of America red curls might look fine on little girls like Letty, but they seem unmanly on a boy.

Ma was bent toward the stove, feeding in a piece of wood, neatly chopped and split by Pa. Her apron was tied in a lopsided bow in the middle of her back over a gray dress that when she bent over showed just the tops of her high shoes. I could see why Pa had taken such a fancy to her. She must have been a beauty when she was young.

I guess she felt me staring at her, because just then she turned around and smiled. I don't know any woman in the world with such a smile. It would charm the gruff off a Billy Goat, that smile. "You must be feeling better," she said, and came over and kissed my forehead. Ordinarily a boy who is nearly eleven would dodge a kiss from his ma, but I knew she meant no harm. It was just her way of taking my temperature. I lay back and let her tuck the quilt up. "Oatmeal this morning?" she asked, so sweetly that I felt tears starting in my eyes. I pulled the quilt up a bit to hide my face. "Or I could do griddle-cakes, if you have the appetite."

Flapjacks for breakfast! She was making a pet of me. I pushed the covers off my face. "Yes, thank you," I said.

She laughed, a sound pleasing as the song of a hermit

thrush. About then it dawned on me that my sickness had turned me into treacle pudding. I couldn't let that happen. But every time I tried to stop thinking about home and how glad I was to be there, my mind would go to Vile, who had none. How was she managing it alone? I tried to tell myself she was better off without that old villain, but she wouldn't know that. What was she eating? Why hadn't I made her take at least a handful of Montpelier crackers last night? The sweet smell of flapjacks on the griddle and sausage in the pan made me think all the more bitterly of some nauseous soup that might well be her only nourishment today.

Today? I sat up so fast, my head spun. "Ma!"

Ma wheeled around from the stove to study me. "What is it, Robbie? What's the matter?"

"Nothing." I shook my head, gently so as not to make my headache worse. Today they'd be sending Zeb to Tyler to stand trial. *For kidnapping and attempted murder.* Not just that, I told myself. He'd practically destroyed Wolcott's Drugstore, hadn't he? I fingered the bandage on my head. My poor head. Hadn't I nearly died?

I lay back down carefully. Let the rascal hang, or rather, let him rot in jail. What did I care? He deserved it, the old drunk. Vile would be better off if she never laid eyes on him again.

But what would happen to her? Where could she go? There were orphanages. I dropped that when scenes from *Oliver Twist* came to mind. Or kindly widows, as in

Huckleberry Finn. I tried to picture Vile with somebody like Aunt Millie. They'd drive each other crazy in a week. I let out a giggle.

Ma turned again, looking a little puzzled, but when I just smiled and shrugged, she turned back to the stove. She's too much of a lady to pry.

Pa would know what to do about Vile. I'd tell him about her. He'd figure out something good. Wouldn't Vile be happier in a warm house with three sure meals a day than in a ruined cabin where you'd freeze even in July?

The family began to gather. Apparently they'd been eating in the parlor while I was sick so as not to disturb me. Beth took note of the flapjacks, snuck a look at me, and sniffed slightly before intercepting Letty at the door to put on her apron for her.

"Flajacks for breffast!" squealed Elliot and clapped his hands. Pa patted his shoulder and nodded at me.

"It appears your mother has killed the fatted calf, on a Wednesday, even."

I knew what the "fatted calf" meant. When the Prodigal Son comes home after wasting all his father's goods, instead of scolding him, the father throws a feast to welcome him. I didn't know quite how to feel, Pa likening me to the Prodigal.

When Ma announced that breakfast was ready, I sat up and made to put my feet on the floor. Pa stopped me. "You can eat your griddlecakes right there, Robbie. The doctor doesn't want you bouncing around for a few days yet." I lay back down. My head was throbbing from just trying to stand. Ma sent Letty to fetch a couple of cushions from the parlor. Then Pa propped me up so I could eat my breakfast from a tray.

At the table Pa said the blessing, adding a thanks to God that I was improving in health and strength. Everybody dug in except Ma, who was watching me like a mother hawk from her position at the stove. "Small bites, Robbie. You have to eat slowly. You haven't had any solid food for a week." My mouth was jammed full of sausage and flapjacks with maple syrup leaking out the corners. I could only nod in answer. "*Small* bites, Robbie, and chew each one."

"He'll be all right, Mother," said Pa. "Now you come sit down and enjoy some yourself." She looked at me doubtfully, but she put another platter of cakes on the table, served herself, and sat down.

It felt lonely watching the five of them gathered around the table eating and talking and me across the room on the daybed with my solitary tray. Maybe it sounds silly, but I felt as far away from them at that moment as I had up at the cabin.

Occasionally, Ma would peer across the table at me and smile as if to ask how I was. But it just made me feel lonelier and less a part of them all to be singled out. I was drifting down past melancholy toward self-pity when Beth said, "I heard they were moving that man to Tyler today."

A shiver went through me. I didn't want to be reminded.

"What man?" Letty asked.

"Da bad man wha' stole Robbie," answered Elliot, proud to be the one who knew the answer.

My stomach lurched. I grabbed the chamber pot and fed it all my breakfast.

The Impossible Occurs

"Robbie!" Both Ma and Pa were beside me in a hop. "Oh, it's all my fault," Ma moaned. "I should have known better than to give him sausage."

"It's all right, Mother." Pa was wiping my face with his big white handkerchief. He put it back in his pocket, gave me a wry smile, and took hold of the chamber pot I was still clutching. "Need this any longer?"

I shook my head and lay back against the parlor cushions.

"It smells bad!" Letty protested.

"I'll take care of it," Pa said, bearing my late lamented breakfast out to the privy.

"Excuse me," Beth said primly. "I seem to have lost my appetite."

"Robbie din' mean to. Di' you, Robbie?" Elliot was leaning anxiously over me.

"No, Robbie didn't mean to be sick," Ma said, watching my face and not Elliot's while she spoke to him. "Now go back to the table and finish your breakfast."

The girls were soon out of the kitchen, leaving Ma still looking worried and guilty and Elliot reaching over to the girls' plates and helping himself to their flapjacks.

Pa brought the chamber pot, scrubbed clean, back in and put it down beside the daybed.

"Pa," I began, not sure how to say what I needed to say.

"Yes, Robbie?"

"The—the man they caught has a girl, a daughter. Is anyone seeing to her while—you know—while—"

Pa sat down on the side of the daybed, smiling as though I'd said a kindly thing. "We surely will take care of her when we find her, but right now no one knows where she is."

"I think—well, they were staying in that old abandoned cabin—"

"Yes, that's what the man said. But Willie and I looked there—"

"It ain't her fault, Pa. She can't help he's her father."

"No." Carefully, he pulled the parlor cushions out from under my back. "No. She can't help that." He patted my shoulder. "Now, you just lie here and get a good rest. Don't you fret about the girl. I'll ask around. Do you know her name?"

"Vile," I said. It felt good to be stretched out flat again.

"Vile?"

"For Violet. Violet Finch."

I tried to keep a picture in my mind of Pa climbing the

hill again like the Good Shepherd looking for the lost lamb. Finding Vile huddled up in the cabin, frightened and alone, and gently persuading her to come home with him, taking her small dirty hand into his big strong clean one— It didn't work. No matter that I'd brought on another headache trying to concentrate on Vile's rescue, by midmorning Pa had come home alone.

"I went up to the cabin again. I'm afraid she's gone— cleared out. There's nothing to suggest that anyone has been there for the last day or so."

I didn't sleep well that night. Why should I have to feel responsible for Vile? She wasn't my care. She wouldn't want to be. I'd nearly got myself killed trying to save her life, and was she grateful? It was plain she didn't want me or anyone else trying to help her. I tossed over to the other side, sending a pain through my skull. She'd come in the middle of the night to ask me for help. . . . But I was hardly in my right mind when she was begging me so pitiful, and she sped away as soon as she heard Pa coming. I really hadn't had a chance to say or do anything.

I turned over again. I must have been groaning out loud, because before long Pa was sitting beside me, putting a cold compress to my forehead.

"Shh—shh. It's all right, Robbie. Just try to lie still and the pain will go away."

His hand felt warm and healing on my head. I wanted to grab it and hold it there, but it seemed a baby—an Elliot—kind of gesture. I kept my arms stiffly by my sides.

After a while he leaned over and kissed my forehead, just as Ma might have. "Can you get back to sleep, do you think?"

I wanted to beg him to stay with me. Instead I said, "Yessir," and he went quietly up the stairs.

Morning came at last. Pa was down as early as Ma, dressed in his Sunday suit. "I'll just take some bread and tea," he said to her. "I have to get on my way." He came over to the daybed before he left, but I pretended to be asleep. He was gone before I realized that it was important that I know where he'd gone.

Carefully, I propped myself up on my elbows, trying to avoid those sudden movements that sent my head to clanging. "Where'd Pa go?" I asked.

"Oh, Robbie. I was hoping you were still asleep."

"Pa. Where did he have to go?"

"To catch the early train," she said.

"Is somebody in the hospital?" Somehow when you're sick yourself, you tend to forget that things happen to other people at the same time. I'd forgot that Pa still had parishioners to think of.

"No. No one's sick. They've called him to testify."

"Testify?" A picture flashed in my head of a big prayer meeting in the city, where Pa would get up like Deacon Slaughter and make announcements about what God was up to. "Testify in Tyler?"

"About the kidnapping," she said gently. "Dr. Blake said you weren't well enough to be a witness yourself, so they called on your father."

"Oh." I lay back down slowly. I had to think. Even Pa thought Zeb had kidnapped me. Well, the bum had nearly killed me. What was the difference? *Thou shalt not bear false witness.*

I reasoned that Pa wouldn't know it was false. He'd only say what he believed to be true. But I knew better. And Vile, wherever she was, knew better. She'd never forgive me if I let my pa send hers to prison for kidnapping. Why hadn't I told Pa the truth? I let out a sigh as long as a train pulling into the depot.

"Are you feeling all right, Robbie?" Ma asked.

"Yeah," I said, my voice strangling in my throat.

I watched the rest of them eat their oatmeal, my head whirling even though I was flat on my back. Was I to be the cause of my father lying in court after laying his hand on the Holy Bible and swearing to tell nothing but the truth? *He doesn't know what the truth is or isn't.* A voice came into my head powerful as though it had come down from Mount Sinai. *But you know the truth, and you let him bear false witness.*

I managed to choke down a little oatmeal with a lot of maple sugar and cream.

"Will you be all right if the girls and I go to the sewing circle this morning, Robbie? We missed it last week—"

All of a sudden it seemed God was clearing the way. "Sure," I said. "I just want to nap this morning, I think."

"If you need anything, just send Elliot down for us, all right?"

I waited until I was sure Ma and the girls were well out of sight of the house. Elliot was on the porch, where Ma had told him to stay in case I needed him. He was playing paper dolls, it sounded like, from the way he kept switching his voice from treble to bass. "Elliot!" I called.

He came at once, running in his lopsided way to my bedside. "Wha's a matter, Robbie? You need me t' get Ma?"

"No. Something else. Will you go upstairs and get me my Sunday suit and cap and my shoes and stockings?"

"Why for, Robbie?"

"I got to get dressed. Pa's in trouble, and I have to help him."

"Pa in trouble?" The idea was uncomprehensible. His eyes were wide as poppies and his mouth agape.

"Don't worry. He'll be all right. Only I have to get dressed." He didn't move. "Please, Elliot. Just go up and get my things. Now!"

He jumped a little at the last word, then hurried to obey.

I got up very slowly and even more slowly walked to the sink. I turned on the spigot and caught a little water in my hands and rubbed my face. Next thing I knew, I was grabbing the front of the sink with both hands. I held on until I stopped swaying. All the time since I'd been hurt, I'd only gotten up to use the chamber pot beside the daybed. Walking across the kitchen floor was about to do me in. I sat down on the nearest chair until my head settled.

"You aw right, Robbie?"

"Yeah," I said, pressing my lips together. "Just put the clothes down on the bed, Elliot. That's all."

"Not even 'Sank you, Elliot'?"

"Oh, sure. Thank you, Elliot." Behind my back I could hear a little grunt of pleasure. "Now go along to the porch and play or—whatever you do."

"I wanna help you, Robbie."

"No, I'm fine. Thank you, though."

"I wanna help you help Pa. Can I?"

"No, Elliot." It would be hard enough for me to pull this off alone. How could I manage if I had to take care of Elliot as well? He had come over to my chair and twisted his head around to put his face right into mine.

"Pleash." He looked as though he was about to burst into tears.

I pulled back away from his face. "Oh, yeah, there is something else you can do."

"Wha', Robbie?"

"Go get my bank off the dresser. We'll need some money."

At the word *we* he broke into a grin and lumbered over to the stairs and thundered up the two flights. I had to figure out something fast, some way to keep him occupied while I did what had to be done. Despite his clumsiness he was back by the time I'd gotten around the table and sat down on the daybed.

"Now"—I lowered my voice to a whisper, making it up as I went along—"your job—your job is to go down to the general store—"

He looked puzzled. "By myshel'?"

"Yeah," I said. "We're going to have to split up at first."

"Wha' I do at da store?"

"You—uh—wait. In case, just in case they show up."

"Who show up?"

"The—the bad men," I blurted out. I looked close to see if I'd scared him. I hadn't meant to.

"Da bad man gone to Tyler."

"Well, one of them has—the worst one. But he's got some bad friends. They're the ones we got to get for Pa."

"Oh." He hesitated, then raised his drooped shoulder a bit so he seemed to be standing up a little straighter. "'kay," he said. "How dey look?"

I had to think fast. What I was trying to do was keep Elliot safely on the porch of the general store until at least dinnertime. I wasn't trying to scare him, for heaven's sake. So I thought of the most impossible description in the world. "They'll be riding in a motorcar," I said.

"Wha'?"

"You know, Elliot. I've told you about them. They're just like buggies, but they don't need a horse."

"How dey go?"

165

"Magic," I said.

"Oh." It was explanation enough. "Wha' I do when dey come?"

I was getting impatient to be rid of him, so I said the first thing that came into my mind. "Catch 'em."

He nodded importantly. "'kay, Robbie."

"Here," I said, shaking two pennies into his hand. "Buy yourself a couple of fireballs to suck while you wait."

"Sank you, Robbie. You good bruver." I think he might have hugged me if I hadn't ducked. "Why *you* goin' get aw dress' up?"

"I have to get dressed in case, you know, just in case they come here."

He looked totally confused, so I began to talk faster. "See, when you catch the bad guys for Pa—boy, he'll be proud, he'll say what a hero you've been—after you catch 'em, you have to bring 'em up here for me to identify, to make sure they the ones that really helped that feller— you know—the feller they took to Tyler."

He nodded his big head seriously. I was relieved he didn't have the sense to ask me how he was supposed to make them come up to the manse. "I wouldn't want those villains to find me lying here in my nightshirt, now would I?"

He giggled.

"Hey! You better get going."

• • •

I had to sit down twice even before I came to pull my stockings up and buckle my stupid knickers. Crikey, but I'll be glad when Ma admits I'm man enough to wear long pants on Sundays. When I leaned down to tie the laces of my shoes, my head spun around so fast, I had to bring my foot up to the bed to get the job done.

Just dressing myself had exhausted me, but I couldn't go puny now. I stood up and held still until the spinning stopped. At the door I had a glimpse of myself in the kitchen mirror. The dratted bandage. I tried on my Sunday cap, but it sat on the top of my bound-up head like a rabbit on a snowdrift. On the porch I grabbed Pa's gardening hat off a peg. It would have to do.

I cannot adequately describe the horrors of that walk. I tried to pretend I was a prisoner, just released from Andersonville Prison after the Great War, making my way home to Vermont. My mind was telling my body to run, but my poor body was crying to lie down and die. Somehow I made it down School Street to West Hill Road, pausing to lean against the Martins' stone wall to catch my breath, praying that none of the neighbor ladies had stayed home from sewing circle. That was all I needed—some nosy woman to come running out to force me back home to bed. Or, worse yet, Rachel Martin to spy me in the state I was in.

When I finally got down the slope to Main Street, I was seen. But it was only a couple of the stonecutters taking a smoke outside the sheds. They stared at me, especially at my strange headgear, but I knew they wouldn't interfere.

It was ten miles from there. When I was young and healthy, I'd done it in under three hours. That day I was slower than a wounded veteran in the Fourth of July parade.

I tried not to remember how far I had to go. Didn't those veterans walk home from way down South somewhere? I kept telling myself just to keep one foot in front of the other, not to think of the distance, just to keep going down the road.

I kept remembering those wounded soldiers. How had they kept marching hour after hour? They sang, didn't they? I tried a chorus of "John Brown's body," but "moldering in the grave" brought to mind that they'd hanged John Brown. It didn't seem lucky to sing about a man who had ended up on the gallows.

During the third verse of "Onward, Christian Soldiers" I heard a great commotion. My first thought was that it was all happening inside my head, that something like a charge of the black powder they use up at the quarry was going off inside my skull. I grabbed my head between both hands, hoping against hope to keep it from exploding right there in the middle of the Tyler road. Then I heard a honk like that of a giant goose right on my rump. Bad head or not, I jumped, I tell you, high as a hound after a treed coon.

"Get out of the middle of the road, you young fool!

Do you want to be run down?"

The thing that had stopped just short of my rear end was a bright red motorcar. This motorcar made the one I'd seen in Tyler look like a toy. It was huge—with lanterns, black leather seats, one behind the other—and it had a wheel to steer with. A man, his face almost as red as the motorcar, was at the wheel. Beside him sat a woman, beautiful as an angel, in a huge hat with netting tied over it and under her chin.

I didn't move an inch. I guess I did look like some kind of fool standing there staring, my mouth wider than a granite quarry. *A motorcar!* There'd never been a motorcar on this road since the blinking things got themselves invented. I couldn't do anything but just stand there and gape. It was the most beautiful machine I had ever laid my eyes on, growling like it was raring to leap up and pounce on the road.

The driver was getting more impatient by the second. "Move, I say. Move."

"Oh, Oliver," said the woman. "He's just a boy. He's probably never seen a motorcar before."

I had, but I wasn't about to argue. I moved, though, to let them pass. "Excuse me," I said.

The machine began to roar and move forward, but as it did so, a figure popped up from the back, waving both arms. "Robbie! Robbie! I catch 'em!"

I did what turned out to be the smartest thing I could have done. I fainted dead away.

The Prodigal Son Returns to the Fold

The next thing I knew, I was lying stretched out in the ditch with three heads hovering over me, blocking out the sun.

"He not dead! He not dead!" Elliot was hollering over the roar of the motor as I came around.

"No, but he's been hurt." The lady was examining my bandage. Pa's garden hat was in her hand. "We're terribly sorry," she said to me. "My husband had no intention—"

"What were you doing wandering out alone in your condition?" the man demanded. "Where are your parents that they'd let you . . ." Abruptly, he turned from me to Elliot. "And you, who are *you*? And *what* were you doing in my motorcar?" He looked at Elliot, not pitying like most people do, but furious. "Why, you little— You must have climbed in when we stopped at the store. I knew we shouldn't stop."

"Shh, Oliver, not now, please. The child's been hurt." She fanned my face with Pa's hat. "Feeling any better?" she asked.

I nodded. It seemed wise not to recover too quickly.

"Well, on your feet, then," the man said. "I suppose we'll have to take you home." He looked at Elliot. "Both of you."

Elliot looked at me, a troubled expression clouding his face. "But dey bad—" he muttered.

"It's all right, Elliot," I whispered quickly. "The bad fellers were in a different car. This one's fine."

The woman helped me to my feet. Elliot tried to dust my knickers and stockings, but I brushed away his hand. I didn't want to try the man's patience further by keeping him waiting.

Between Elliot and the lady, I managed to climb up into the back seat. Elliot clambered up after me and made to crouch down between the seats. "It's okay, Elliot. You can ride the rest of the way on the seat by me."

"Where do you boys live, then?" the driver asked once we were all settled in the motorcar.

"Tyler," I said.

Elliot poked me in the ribs. "Robbie," he whispered. "Da's a lie."

I ignored him. "Tyler," I said louder.

"Both of you?"

"We're brothers," I said. Elliot grinned proudly.

"Where on God's earth is Tyler?" the man asked.

"Straight down this road, sir." I mouthed the word *Pa* at Elliot. He nodded solemnly. "Just a little way." The driver craned around and gave me a look. I didn't blink, so he eased forward.

The road to Tyler is bumpy and dusty, but I hardly noticed. I felt like I had hitched a ride in Elijah's chariot on a straight path to the Pearly Gates. I was riding in a motorcar! The one thing I had wanted most to do before the world went bust, and God had let me do it. Moreover, God hadn't given me just a ride, He had provided a saving help in my time of trouble. The Reverend Pelham could have his white robes and golden crowns and choirs of angels; I was in Heaven already.

I grabbed Elliot's hand. "Can you believe it, Elliot? You and me? We're riding in a genuine motorcar!"

"Is dat good?"

"It's a miracle!" I yelled over the racket of the motor. "A genuine miracle!"

"Wheeee!" cried Elliot. Then he leaned over and kissed my hand.

And do you know? From that very moment I stopped all pretense of being an apeist and signed on as a true believer for all eternity. How could I not? God had worked a personal miracle especially for me.

The main street of Leonardstown becomes, at the town limits, the Tyler road, and roughly ten miles later, Main Street, Tyler. By the time less than half those miles had rolled under the rubber wheels, our driver was getting audibly impatient. Seems they were trying to get to

Burlington and had no idea how they had got on this "back road to nowhere." I couldn't see why anyone would complain. We were whizzing (well, rattling is more accurate) down the road by at least fifteen miles an hour. Tyler is hardly more than fifty miles from Burlington. He'd be there before suppertime. I kept my observations to myself.

I can't tell you how it saddened me to reach the city limits. No matter that every rock and rut along the way jarred my poor brain against my pitiful skull; I wanted to go on riding in that heavenly chariot forever. When I saw the courthouse, however, I pulled myself together. Duty demanded it.

"Right here," I said. "Thank you for the ride."

He stopped smack in front of the courthouse. I could see people beginning to gather from all directions, coming to stare at the motorcar. I was briefly tempted to wait, so that it would be *me* sitting in the back seat that they would see and envy, but I put old Satan behind me. "C'mon, Elliot," I said, climbing down carefully so as not to jar my head. "Thank the nice lady and man."

"Sank you," he said sweetly.

"You live at the *courthouse*?" The man was about to get riled at me again, but he saw all the people come crowding near, reaching out to touch his treasured vehicle. He was anxious then to be rid of me and Elliot and move out of danger.

The lady waved at us. "Take care of yourselves, boys," she called as they pulled away from the curb. We waved back. Then I grabbed Elliot's hand, and we started up the long flight of granite steps to the courthouse door where my duty lay in wait.

Elliot opened the door for me, looking anxiously at my face for signs of fainting. I was dizzy as a top, but I managed to smile. "Now, we go in there," I said, pointing at the heavy double doors that I figured must open into the courtroom itself. "I think Pa's in there."

I knew at once who was the judge and who were the jury. I could see the back of poor Zeb's head bent over a table at the front. There were maybe thirty or so people sitting in what looked like church pews. Before I could locate Pa, he spotted us standing at the back of the big room. He came hurrying from where he had been sitting. "Robbie, Elliot, what on earth . . . ?"

"Shh," warned a large man standing near the door. "No talking in here."

Pa guided us back into the vestibule. "What are you boys doing here?" He looked at me closely. "You've no business being out of bed, Robbie."

"We ride da motorcar," Elliot said, but Pa wasn't listening.

"Here," he said, taking me by the elbow. "At least sit down." He led me over to a long wooden bench. I was glad to sink down on it.

"Robbie, what in the name of Heaven—?"

"Pa." How could I explain everything? "I got to testify."

He didn't interrupt me, just waited patiently for me to figure out how to put the words together. "First. I was never kidnapped. So if they hang him, it would be—it would be just like I'd murdered him."

"Then the note . . . ?"

"It—it was kind of a . . . joke." My head was hanging nearly to my boots. "No one was meant to see it. It—it was sort of a mistake that it got into Zeb's pocket at all."

He could tell there was more to the story, but he put his hand on my shoulder to indicate I didn't have to go into *all* the gory details just then. "We'll talk about that later," he said. "The pressing matter is what will happen to Mr. Finch today. I don't think they plan to hang him, Robbie, but no matter. If there was no kidnapping, the judge must be told."

I looked up into his kind, honest face. I bet Abraham Lincoln didn't have as good and honest a face as my pa. The problem with such a face is it makes the other feller have to search his own false soul, so I bared mine. "Truth is," I said, "I run away. After I dunked Ned Weston, I was afraid . . . Pa, the truth is I nearly drowned Ned Weston. I was scared—and shamed." I could feel tears starting behind my eyes. I didn't want to cry like a weakling just when I was trying so hard to be strong and do what was good and proper.

He sat down on the bench beside me and put his arm around my shoulder. "Thank you for telling me, Robbie. You're right, we need to talk to the judge straightaway."

Standing with Pa before the judge in his little back room, I wanted to confess everything. I started with Mabel Cramm's bloomers and how I turned into an apeist, wanting nothing but the pleasures of life before the end come. How I stole vegetables from my own parents and how I had succumbed to anger and nearly drowned Ned Weston.

About then the judge interrupted me. "I don't need to know everything that's on your conscience, son. That's between you and your Maker. I just need to know if you were kidnapped by Zebulon Finch."

"No, sir, I was not."

"Then the note they found on him was something of a hoax?"

It seemed wise to agree.

"But he did attack you?"

"Yessir, he hit me, but that was partly my fault. Me and Vile—Violet Finch, that's his daughter—we stole his booze. He had gone down to get some more."

"From the drugstore?"

"He favors Willerton's Digestive Remedy. You may not know, sir, but Willerton's is mighty near pure alcohol."

"I see," he said, something like a smile playing around his mouth.

"The booze just makes him crazy, and really, I attacked him first."

He looked at me thoughtfully. "*You* were the aggressor?

Are you saying that Mr. Finch hit you in self-defense?" It was clear he didn't believe me.

"See," I said, "I thought he was fixing to hurt Vile Violet—so I jumped him. He was just striking back. He didn't mean to really hurt me. I know he didn't. It was more or less an accident."

"I see." The judge exchanged glances with Pa, who nodded his head. His Honor called one of the constables and told him to take Elliot and me out to the bench in the vestibule and then go buy us each a bottle of Moxie, which we couldn't drink in the courtroom but we could out on the bench where we'd sat before.

"Ed?"

I nearly dropped my Moxie. "Vile! Where you been?"

"Around," she said. She stared at my drink.

"Here," I said. "Have some. It's right tasty."

She took a long drag from my bottle. I could see she was reluctant to hand it back.

"Nah, you keep it. I had plenty."

"You wan' mine?" Elliot held out his bottle.

She nodded. Vile finished off both bottles of Moxie without hardly taking a breath. "Thanks for coming," she said, giving me and Elliot the empty bottles. "I was just listening in there before I came out here." She jerked her head at the courtroom door. "I think they're going to let him go."

"Good," I said. "That's good."

"Who's your pal?" she asked, nodding at Elliot.

"It's my brother," I said. "Say hello to Violet, Elliot."

"Hey, Bi-let," Elliot said. "How you?"

"I'm doing great," Vile said. "Just great, thanks." It was the first time I'd seen her really smile.

My head was throbbing fierce, and all I wanted to do was stretch out on the bench and go to sleep, but I was determined not to go puny in front of Vile. It seemed years before the doors finally opened and people begun to filter out of the courtroom. The ones from Leonardstown smiled at me and Elliot, gave Vile a stare, and hurried on out. Pa and Zeb were about the last ones out the double doors. Zeb was kind of shuffling from one foot to the other, not daring to raise his head.

"It's all right, Paw," Vile said. "Ed don't hold nothing against you."

"Ed?" Pa looked puzzled.

"It—it was kind of a game," I said. "Vile—Violet knows good and well that my real name is *Robbie*, don't you, Violet?"

"Huh?" She gave me one of her sharpest looks. "Oh, yeah. Sure, *Robbie*."

"Violet," Pa said, "you and your father will be coming back to Leonardstown with us." He pulled his watch out of his pocket. "But we're going to have to step on it if we're going to make the last train."

"Robbie cain' walk too good," Elliot said.

"Want a piggyback, son?"

As embarrassing as it was to climb on Pa's back like I was a five-year-old, I was grateful to Elliot. Vile or no Vile, I'd done all the walking I could manage for one day.

The End and Beginning of Many Things

The court put Pa in charge of Zeb for the next three months. Pa got him a job working at the Leonardstown hotel, where they could have a room and three meals a day. The judge had said Zeb could remain in Pa's custody as long as he went to work every day and didn't touch alcohol. The damage to Wolcott's Drugstore was considerable, but Mr. Wolcott agreed that Zeb could pay him a bit out of his salary every week to help make restitution.

If there was a sheriff on Zeb's tail, the officer never appeared. By September Vile had stopped snatching every handbill in sight. Seems she couldn't read well enough on the run to see if they pertained to Zeb or not, so she stole them all, just in case.

I thought at that point that everything was going to end happily ever after, but it didn't quite work out that way, and since I am back on the Ten Commandments, I have to tell you the truth of things. First of all, school opened like always. For me it wasn't as bad as I'd feared.

I sat right behind Rachel Martin again. Miss Bigelow, despite the business about the snake, decided to come back another year. She'd gotten prettier over the summer. I wasn't the only one who thought so. Willie even remarked on it out loud. She was nice, too. Miss Bigelow, I mean. Rachel Martin continued to ignore me.

Miss Bigelow was especially good to Vile, who she never failed to address as Violet and made everyone else do the same. It didn't make a bit of difference, though. Vile cordially hated going to school. She was so far behind every other eleven-year-old that she claimed it was like drinking pure bile to recite her lessons. She used to say that school was worse than jail. "And here I was so worried about poor old Paw getting caged up, and I'm the one who's lost their freedom."

Willie and me tried to make life easier for her. We really did. Even Pa helped. He offered to give her extra tutoring, but Vile claimed she had something that made her break into hives if she got too close to a preacher. I told her that was nonsense, but she showed me these red spots on her arms and said, "See!" I suspect they were bedbug bites, but I decided to leave it be. Next thing she'd claim she couldn't sleep in a regular bed.

Elliot was crazy about her, but Elliot likes everybody. The interesting thing is that Vile liked him back. Sometimes she would come up to the house not to see me but just to play paper dolls with Elliot and Letty. It was the only time I ever saw her acting like a regular little girl.

Anyhow, the first snow fell in October soon after Zeb's three-month parole was up. They disappeared the night after it snowed, heading, I guess, for warmer territory. They were originally from somewhere farther south. Anyhow, I got a postal card from Vile at Christmastime written in smudged pencil. They had made their way as far as Massachusetts, hopping trains. Zeb was mostly behaving himself, she said. She herself was working in a mill, which she didn't mind at all since no one made her recite lessons in a mill. I mustn't worry. She had taken the primer that Pa had given her and was teaching herself. Couldn't I tell how much her writing had improved even without her having to go to school? She spelled *writing* as *ritin*. And that was about the best spelling on the card. I spent more than an hour puzzling out what she was trying to say. It made me furious that she didn't know what was good for her. She could have had a swell life here in Leonardstown with us, but she threw it away.

It made me sad, too. Even if she was happier in Massachusetts, she was like a buddy to Willie and Elliot and me. We all miss her. Now that I'm back to being a Christian, I pray she'll come back. She hasn't so far.

The whole town was planning to stay up on December the thirty-first and watch the new century dawn. Deacon Slaughter and Mr. Weston had already determined that our celebration would be simple and in the good taste befitting a God-fearing town in Vermont.

182

Unlike those festivities being advertised in the larger cities, Leonardstown would tolerate no raucous behavior, drunkenness, or dancing in the street. (Not that anyone would be tempted to dance on a street of packed snow in their winter boots.) There was to be a band concert in the town hall at seven P.M., followed by prayer meetings in the individual churches. The plan was that everyone would assemble on the green afterward and say a proper farewell to the nineteenth century and welcome the twentieth. Willie and I had stuffed our pockets with strings of firecrackers and matches in honor of the occasion. But when the concert and prayer meetings were over, it was still not ten-fifteen and the temperature was plunging faster than a wild goose full of buckshot.

People stood around, shuffling their freezing toes and mumbling. After a while Mrs. Weston remarked rather loud that anybody with any sense would go home and welcome in the new century in the comfort of their own homes. The crowd began to drift away after that. We young ones complained, but we were not listened to. Maybe someone had gotten wind of those firecrackers and was scared one of us fellers would burn our britches or worse.

If anyone but me was thinking about it being almost the End of the Age, they didn't say so. It wasn't even mentioned during the prayer meeting. I wondered if people had forgotten so quickly all the excitement over the potential apocalypse when Reverend Pelham was here in June, or if they just didn't want to dwell on the possibility.

We sat in the kitchen. Ma made us hot sassafras tea and Pa popped corn. We had a good time for a while until Letty fell asleep in her chair. Then everyone started to yawn. As it turned out, only Pa and me could keep our eyes open past eleven-thirty.

"Come on, Robbie," he said, consulting his watch, "why don't we greet the new age outside among the stars."

We put on our coats and caps and high boots. Pa grabbed the lantern from the kitchen table. The two of us tromped through the snow across the back yard to the edge of Webster's pasture. It was bitter cold, as it tends to be when the sky is perfectly clear. The stars were sparkling and winking like they were dancing for joy. We craned our necks back to stare. A shooting star sped across the dome of the sky and disappeared behind the mountains.

"Pa," I said, "do you think—do you think it will all be over soon?"

"What will be over, Robbie?"

"The world. Do you think it's coming to an end?"

He didn't laugh. "We can't know that sort of thing for sure, son. But my hunch is that this old earth will be here a long time after we are." He was quiet for a minute. Then he added, "I think the world's at a sort of beginning, myself."

"A beginning?"

"Lots of things, things we can't even dream of today, will be happening in your lifetime. The world is changing so fast on us. Telephones, electricity, motorcars—who knows? You might live long enough to see flying machines."

I looked up at the stars and tried to imagine myself like a shooting star, flying up there in a motorcar with wings. Nothing seemed impossible anymore.

"I pray it will be a good century," he went on. "I want my children and my grandchildren to grow up in a world where people have learned to think with their minds and hearts and not with weapons of destruction. But I don't know, the human race being what it is . . ."

I shivered. He put his free arm around me and drew me close. "Pa," I said after a bit, "let's ring it in." I waited for him to say no.

Instead he said, "Last one to the church is a rotten egg!" He thrust the lantern into my hand and took off down the hill, retracing his own tracks in the snow so he could go faster. I followed after, holding the lantern high and stepping carefully into his footprints. He was waiting for me on the church porch, smiling and out of breath. We went in together.

"Don't turn the bell over!" he warned.

"I won't!" Only greenhorns who don't know how to

185

ring proper pull the rope so hard it makes the bell turn over. I took hold of the rope. Pa fit his big hands in between mine, and we began to pull.

High above us from the steeple, the bell of the Congregational church clanged across the valley, pealing out a joyful welcome to the twentieth century.